ARTISTIC LOVE IN THE PSYCH WARD

REGINA ANN FAITH

ISBN: 9781686436598

Library of Congress Control Number:

Edited by Jenna B. Neece

Cover Design by Diana T. Calcado, www.triumphcovers.com

First Printed Edition, 2019.

Jesus:

Thank You for the ability to use my gifts and talents to impact and inspire people from all walks of life.

For my mom:

Thank you for the pearls of wisdom. Love you and miss you so much. RIP.

For my husband to be:

I don't know if we have or haven't met yet. This is a glimpse into what I'm called to do. I pray you pick up this book and see the words on these pages as beautiful and inspiring. I love you so much! Let's make beautiful, inspiring creativity together.

My heart is overflowing with a good theme;
I recite my composition concerning the King;
My tongue is the pen of a ready writer. ***(Psalm 45:1)***

Even Though Your Wounds Are Not Your Fault, Your Healing Is Still Your Responsibility. ***(Unknown)***

1

MORNING OF MOURNING

It was the morning of March 28th. She remembered it so well. There was an overcast sky, and the clouds were dark and gray. She had just woken up, took a shower, and was getting ready to go to school that morning when she felt a heaviness in her heart. She shook it off as maybe her period was coming, and her hormones were out of whack. That day, she wore the dark-colored flare jeans that she brought at H&M's and a flowy Bohemian style floral top. Her hair was a curly fro atop of her head. She put a butterfly clip in a few curls she had pulled back. For footwear, she opted for low tan wedges. She wanted to feel unlike the day felt, as well as the way her emotions felt. With spring upon her, she wanted to feel light and airy, not dark and gloomy.

"Rain, breakfast is ready," yelled her mom from downstairs in the kitchen. She could smell the aroma of the bacon, eggs, toast, pancakes, and cream of wheat. She was starving and couldn't wait to eat breakfast. Her mom never failed to cook a big breakfast for her as she went to school. She always said, "Nutrition equals brainpower."

"Coming," she yelled back downstairs as she grabbed her Vera Bradley book bag, packed with her notebook and paint supplies. She checked herself out in the mirror one last time, and then she headed downstairs.

Her mom was beautiful as always. Today, she had on a navy blue business suit and heels with a white blouse. Her dreadlocked hair was pulled back in a small neat bun, her make-up, natural and light. Every day after Rain left for school, her mom left for work as a receptionist in a lawyer's office.

"Morning, honey," her mom said as she proceeded to hug and kiss her on the cheek.

"How was your night?" she continued. "Here I put your plate on the table."

"Thanks, mom! It was fine. I slept well. Ready to take on the day," she said.

As she sat down to eat, she still couldn't shake that heaviness in her heart. She felt that this day would be forever etched in her memory, but she didn't mention what she was feeling to her mother because she didn't want to worry her.

"So, how arc you this morning?" she asked her mom.

"Fine, love, I'm fine. It's such a dreary day. I hope it clears before I leave for work. I dislike that I have to drive in this weather," she stated. "You promise to drive safely too, okay honey?"

"I will," she reassured her. Once she finished her breakfast, she kissed her goodbye, grabbed her coat and umbrella, and headed out the door.

Her college was not too far from her house. It took fifteen to twenty minutes to drive there. She had k-love blaring on her radio, and her car windows slightly cracked to get a breeze. It was a peaceful ride, despite her uneasy feeling.

The first class of the day was Intro to Art with Mr. Duncan. He was a middle-aged man with a very eclectic look. You could tell he was an artist at first glance. They were studying Impressionism art, and their homework was to look up an artist that did impressionistic art and write a two-page paper on the artist. Everyone was to present their paper to the entire class and explain what they learned about the artist they chose. Following this assignment, the students were to paint an impressionistic portrait.

"This is due in two weeks," Mr. D told the class as they all were packing up to leave. "Class dismissed."

She had a thirty-minute break before her next class, so she decided to go to the library to try and find books on Impressionistic art to get some ideas on what she could draw for her project. As soon as she headed to the library, her phone vibrated. She stopped and sat at a nearby bench. She had a missed call from her mom, and she left a voicemail. She thought that was strange. Her mom never called her at school unless it was something urgent. Her hands were shaking as she dialed the voicemail. Her mom sounded like she had just finished crying. "Honey, please come home. I have something to tell you." *Was what she was feeling this morning true? Did something awful happen with dad?* Millions of thoughts raced through her mind. She emailed her professor stating that she had an emergency situation at home and couldn't make it to class. She told him she would make up the work later.

She gathered her things, rushed to her car, and took a few deep breaths before starting the engine. She wanted to drive in silence just to listen to her own thoughts, but something told her turn on the radio. Blessings by Laura Story came on, and tears welled up in her eyes. Next up was God Only Knows by For King and Country, and more tears flowed. It was by the grace of God she got home safely because she couldn't see the road due to her crying.

As soon as she reached her driveway, she put her car in park, turned off the engine, and took another deep breath. She got out of her car and walked up to the door in what seemed like slow motion. She didn't want to believe that her thoughts from this morning could be a reality. Her mom opened the door and greeted her with the longest hug imaginable.

"What's wrong mom? What happened? Is dad ok?" She needed answers.

"Honey, dad's fine. It's your grandparents," she said slowly.

"What! Are they ok?" she asked.

"No, honey. They were in a car accident, and both died," her mom said somberly.

Rain couldn't believe what she was hearing. She broke down crying. Her mom reached for her and embraced her again. They cried together and remembered the good times they had with Nani & Pop-Pop.

The next morning, she woke up to red puffy eyes. While looking in the bathroom mirror, and she noticed that she looked like she had just been punched in the eyes. She proceeded to splash warm water on her face to try and ease the puffiness, but it barely even worked. She decided to take a long, hot shower since she still had the clothes on she wore yesterday. After her shower, she got dressed, in simple, casual sweats. She emailed her professors and told them she would be out of class for a while and that she was taking a voluntary leave of absence to deal with the death of her grandparents.

After emailing them, she went down to the kitchen where she saw her mom and dad conversing about funeral arrangements for her grandparents. She bypassed them, got some cereal and milk, and went to the living room couch to eat breakfast while she watched some tv.

"Honey?" her parents called. "Did you contact your professors about being off for a few days?"

"I did, and I've decided to take a leave of absence from college," she replied.

"Are you sure, honey? It will set you back from graduating on time," her mom questioned her.

"I'm sure. I have to take this time to focus on being with you guys. School can wait," she explained.

"We are going this weekend to start clearing out their house. Will you be okay here by yourself, or do you want to come with us?"

"No, I will be fine. You guys go," she said.

"We will only be gone for the weekend. If you need us, call."

"Will do, mom. I love you guys," she proceeded to hug them both.

"We love you too."

* * *

After they said their goodbyes for the weekend, she was left alone to deal with the pain of losing her grandparents. Her Nani and PopPop gave her the nickname Rainbow because even as a little girl, art had a huge part in her life. They saved all the pictures she drew them as a little girl and into her teenage years, and they put them in a book titled "Rainbow of Portraits." They came to every art gallery display that she had from elementary all throughout high school. They were always her biggest fans, and they believed she would have her art displayed in a huge gallery one day, and that they would have been there to support her. As she thought about all these memories, tears started to stream down her face. *Now, they will never get to see her art in a gallery,* she thought. *They would never get to see one of her pieces of art sell. They would never get to see her get married or have children of her own.* It all hit her like a ton of bricks, and she didn't want to live without them. Actually, she didn't know how she was going to live without them.

The next morning, she decided to stream church online, as she waited for her parents to arrive. It was a great message on how to deal with grief. *Such a timely word,* she thought. After the church service finished, she took a shower, got dressed, and headed downstairs to get something to eat. As soon as she stepped onto the last step towards the kitchen, she heard keys jingling in the door. Her parents were home, and they brought with them, bags and a large suitcase.

"Hey, guys. How was your weekend?" she asked.

"Bittersweet. Your grandparents will be truly missed. Going through their belongings brought a flood of grateful memories of the times we shared with them," her dad said.

"Yes, it was bittersweet," her mom echoed his sentiments.

"We have a few things that your Nani and PopPop would have loved for you to have," her mom motioned to a bag full of books. She pulled out one of the books, and immediately, Rain knew what it was.

"My 'Rainbow Portrait' book," she gasped. She held it close to her chest and whispered, "Thank you, mom."

"You're welcome, sweetie. I know this book means a lot to you as you would want to pass it on to your children one day," she explained. "Here's an old bible as well. My mom and dad had quite a few, and I knew you would enjoy looking through their note markings and prayers written in it," she elaborated.

"Oh, thank you, mom. I love it," Rain exclaimed.

* * *

April 1st was the day that the mourning continued. *Or had it just begun?* Rain and her parents entered the church that her Nani and PopPop grew up attending and married in. It was all decorated with white lilies, Nani's favorite flower. PopPop's favorite color was green, so the guestbook was green as well as other little touches of green throughout the church. The church was stunning, stain glass windows, and a cross standing behind the pulpit. On display were pictures of her grandparents when they were young, dating, and married. There were also pictures of Sade, Rain's mom, with them when she was a baby, toddler, teenager, and so forth. At the request of Rain, they displayed the "Rainbow Portrait," book for the last time. She knew her grandparents loved her art, and it wouldn't have been right to not display the book they so proudly made as a keepsake.

The funeral was short and sweet. Rain hadn't known the impact her grandparents had in the community in which they lived. They were well-loved by everyone, and the turnout was a testament to that. Rain and her parents went to the gravesite after the funeral procession. Her grandparents wanted to be buried next to one another. The funeral-goers, Rain, and her parents paid their final respects. The pastor of the church said the eulogy, and everyone placed flowers and cards on their caskets. It was a beautiful tribute to two well-loved members of the community.

On the drive home, it was silent. Rain and her parents were trying to process the day, in their own ways. They each wanted to silently ponder how life would go on without Nani and PopPop.

2

A NEW DAY DAWNING

Four months after her grandparents' death, Rain decided to return back to college. At this time, she wanted to take four classes to get ahead and make up for the time off. She decided to take two art classes, an English class, and a psychology class. She was ready to make her grandparents proud. She knew they would have wanted her to finish college and graduate.

Classes started back up in two weeks, and Rain had to go to her college to pick up her schedule. As she walked into the registrar's office, she saw a long line and tons of students gathered in line to pick up their schedules. She got in one line which seemed to take forever just to get to the front. Once she got to the front, she told the lady her name and major. The lady then typed something in the computer and pressed print. After a few seconds, the lady handed Rain her schedule. She was excited about the two art classes she chose to take, Intro to Abstract Art and Artists of the 1900s. She couldn't wait to learn more about her craft while taking these classes. As she turned to leave, a guy accidentally bumped into her, knocking their schedules to the floor.

"Sorry," the guy said, bending to pick up one of the schedules.

"It's okay," Rain said, bending to pick up the other schedule, surveying it. "I think this is your schedule," she said, handing it to him.

"Thank you, and I think this is yours," he handed the schedule to her. "My name is Zachary," he said

"My name is Rain. It's nice to meet you," she added.

"Likewise. I noticed we have the same art class, Intro to Abstract Art," he stated.

"Oh, we do?" she questioned as she looked down at her schedule.

"We do," Zachary said as he showed her his schedule.

"That's awesome. Are you an art major?" she asked

"No, I'm a computer science major. I'm taking this as an elective requirement."

"Oh, art is my major, and I'm excited to take this class."

"Maybe you can teach me a thing or two about mixing colors," he said jokingly.

"Well, I've got to get ready to go. I will see you in class," she added.

"Of course. It was nice meeting you. See you in two weeks," he said as they parted ways.

Rain left the registrar's office and got in her car to drive to her house. She was excited to continue her studies after a four-month hiatus. During those four months away from school, she continued to draw and paint, even though she was going through a difficult time. It was her escape. She took a picture of her grandparents out of the memory book from their funeral, and she committed to draw it as a gift to her parents. When she presented them with the painting, they were so excited. The painting now hangs in the living room above the couch.

She pulled into her driveway, turned off her car, and walked up to the front door to unlock it. When she opened the door and walked inside, she peeked in the kitchen and saw her mother making dinner.

"Hi, Mom. How was work?" she asked.

"Fine, it was fine. How about your day? How was it?"

"It was good. I just came from picking up my class schedule since classes start in two weeks," Rain added.

"Yes, that's right. Are you ready? Maybe we can go shopping, to pick out some cute outfits for school," her mom suggested.

"That would be great. I would love a mom-daughter day," she exclaimed.

"Is tomorrow good?"

"It's perfect. Tomorrow is perfect," she said as she hugged her mom. "Where's dad?" she added.

"He's still at work. He had to finish tying up some loose ends at the bank," her mother explained. "He'll be home soon though."

"What's for dinner? It smells so good!" Rain asked.

"Shepherd's pie."

"Yum!" Rain said hungrily

Her mom continued cooking as Rain left the kitchen and went to her room.

Rain's room was her sanctuary, filled with her drawings

and paintings. She has tons of notebooks and sketchbooks on her desk. On her easel, there was a painting she was working on. In a box under her bed, she had put her grandparent's bible, the "Rainbow's Portrait" book, and an almost half-filled journal. She grabbed the box from under her bed, pulled out her journal, and opened it to the first entry. She purchased the journal to document her feelings about the death of her grandparents. The first entry was about the day her mother told her the news of her grandparent's death. It was a day she would never forget. She would treasure this journal for a long as she lived. She read the first entry, and then closed her journal. She gently placed it back into the box, closed the lid, and slid it back under her bed. She decided to head back downstairs to see if dinner was ready.

"Mom, is dinner ready? I'm starving," Rain said.

"Yes, honey. I fixed you a plate. It's in the microwave," she told her.

"Thanks," she said as she went to get the food out of the microwave.

She and her mom had sat down at the table to eat when the front door opened and Micah, Rain's dad, walked in.

"Hey, sorry, I'm late. Work was calling," he said, kissing Sade softly, and then he kissed Rain on her forehead. "What's for dinner, darling?" he asked.

"Shepherd's pie. Here, you sit, I'll fix you a plate," Sade said.

"Thanks, darling, you're the best."

Rain watched as her mother fixed her father's plate. She wanted a love like they had. Growing up, she rarely saw them argue, and if they did, they would come to some type of compromise. Early on in their marriage, they decided that they were in this for life. They wanted to be the example for their daughter that marriage is forever and doesn't have to consist of bickering and nagging like most of the couples they knew.

Rain was very grateful to have grown up with such positive role models for marriage.

"This is excellent honey," Micah told his wife, between bites of the shepherd's pie.

"Thank you," she gushed as she finished the last few bites of her food. "So how was your evening at work?"

"It was okay. I finished up on an account I did for a client," he said. "I'm kind of tired, so I'm going to go to bed after I help you clean the kitchen."

He got up and started putting the dishes from the sink into the dishwasher. Sade got up and started to wipe down the table and countertops. Rain went and emptied the trashcan. They all worked to make sure the kitchen was spotless before going to bed.

The next morning, Rain woke up excited to have her mom-daughter day. She got dressed in black palazzo pants with silver stars on them and an oversized black shirt. For shoes, she went with her black and silver vans. She then went downstairs to grab breakfast. She opted for almond milk and two packets of chocolate chips muffins from Little Debbie's. After she ate, she decided to turn on the tv to watch some shows while waiting for her mom. Fifteen minutes into the show, she heard her mother coming down the stairs. Her mother was wearing a jogging suit and tennis shoes, her dreads pulled back in a ponytail.

"Hey, you ready to go?" she asked.

"Of course! Let's go," she said as she turned off the tv.

Her mom grabbed a quick granola bar as they both headed out the door.

They arrived at the mall in fifteen minutes. Traffic was light and moving quickly. Once at the mall, they stopped in Rain's favorite store, Altar'd State. Being in this store was like heaven for her. She bought a few tops and skirts. She also brought some accessories, earrings, necklaces, and hair clips. This was the only store she looked forward to going to. Although being with her mother on this day was perfect, she could be in any store. After they shopped a little more, they decided to go to the food court to get some food.

In the upstairs food court, there were a variety of different fast food restaurants, from McDonald's to Chick-Fil-A and everything in between. Rain decided to go with Chick-Fil-A and got a chicken sandwich, waffle fries, and a fruit punch. Her mom, on the other hand, chose to go with Pizza. She got two slices of pepperoni pizza with extra cheese and a soda. When they each got their food, they searched for a table to sit at. The mall was busy with people shopping. And in the food court, there were tables full of people taking a break from shopping to fill their empty stomachs. Rain and her mother finally found a table and sat down to eat. After eating a few bites, they broke their silence.

"So, are you ready for school or at least excited about your classes?" her mom asked.

"Yes, I'm ready to go back. It's been a long break. I need to get back, so I can graduate on time," Rain said.

"I know Nani and PopPop would be proud of you. You

held us together during this whole ordeal," she said. "Your presence in their lives made a great lasting memory. I know they loved you so much."

"I loved them and will miss them so much. That's why I have to graduate and have my drawings and paintings displayed in an art gallery one day," Rain explained

"You will, honey. You will make them proud, and you will make us proud as well," her mom told her.

They finished up the last few bites of their food, gathered their trash, and threw it in the nearest can. They then gathered their shopping bags and purses, and they walked towards the elevator. Rain pushed the elevator button, and she and her mom waited ten seconds until the elevator rose to their floor. Once the flood of people stepped out, Rain and her mom stepped inside, and the doors closed. Inside, they could view the mall from each angle. They saw people hurrying about, sitting on benches talking, and a bunch of people just standing around. Soon the elevator came to a stop on the first floor, and the doors opened. Rain and her mother stepped out. They decided it was time to go. They'd shopped, ate, and now they were both exhausted.

"Thanks for spending the day with me," Rain told her mom as she was driving them home.

"No problem. I loved our mom-daughter day. We must do this more often," she added.

Soon they arrived in the driveway. They gathered their belongings and stepped out of the car. Rain's mother unlocked the front door went in and put her shopping bags down. Rain followed with her bags and took them to her room.

Rain's father was sitting on the couch watching TV when she came back down from her room. She went over to him, and she hugged him tightly. "I love you, daddy," she gushed.

He hugged her back and said, "I love you too sweetie. How was the mom-daughter day?"

"It was great. We had a blast," she said excitedly.

"That's good to hear. I'm glad you had a great time," he said.

"What did you do all day?"

"Just relaxed. It feels like I work so much. I don't get a day off to myself, so I just relaxed."

"You deserved it!" she said. "You know, you deserve a day of relaxation too."

Meanwhile, while Rain was conversing with her dad, her mom went to take the shopping bags she had to her room. When she came back down, she joined Rain and her husband on the couch. They decided to watch a movie together. Having time to bond was a top priority in their family.

Finally, it was the week school was to start back, and Rain had bought her school supplies and a new book bag. She decided on another Vera Bradley bag. She packed her bag the night before the start of her classes. Her class Intro to Abstract Art and her psychology class was on Monday and Wednesday. The other art class, Artists of the 1900s, and her English class was Tuesday and Thursday. She chose to have

Friday off to study and catch up on other class work she might be given.

Monday morning, she woke up excited to start her classes. She took a shower and got dressed. She wore the bell-sleeved top she brought at Altar'd State and a long black shirt. For shoes, she decided on black flats, since she'd be walking from class to class. She grabbed her new Vera Bradley book bag and headed downstairs to the kitchen.

In the kitchen, she grabbed a cereal bar and put some orange juice in a thermos. Before heading out though, she wrote her mom a note telling her to have a great day, and that she loved her.

It was going to be a great day. She was determined of that. While driving to her college, per usual, she blasted K-love, but instead of having the windows cracked, she had the heat on. It was almost fall, and the leaves were starting to turn colors. There was a cool breeze blowing.

She parked her car in a parking space and got out. The campus buzzed with students, new and returning. Confident students strutted to their classes and novice students looking at their schedules to find out where their classes were. Her first class, Intro to Abstract Art, was at 9:00 am in the Art building adjacent to the library. She walked into the class and sat down. As soon as she sat down, the other students started to file in the class. She wondered if Zachary was coming. She remembered him from the day she got her schedule. As soon as she thought that, he came strolling in.

"Hey! Excuse me, I forgot your name," he said.

"My name is Rain. Hi, Zach, I remembered your name," she said jokingly.

"Good memory. I'm impressed," he answered. "Are you going to teach me how to mix colors?" he asked.

"If you want me to. It's really simple actually," she answered back. As soon as she finished answering Zachary, in walked the professor.

The professor was a short lady, probably in her early 50's, with bleach blonde hair. She was wearing a button-down blouse, black slacks, and black heels. She introduced herself to the class as Professor Maggart, or Professor M. She explained the syllabus and went over each point, making sure to cover all the basics. Then, she explained the first assignment to the class. She wanted them to write about an abstract artist and recreate one of their paintings. She told the class to pair up to work on the project, that it was due in four weeks, and it was to be presented in front of the class.

Zachary turned to Rain and said, "You want to partner up?"

"Sure. It should be fun. I can finally show you how to mix that paint," she smirked.

"Ok," he smiled back at her. "When are you free to start working on the project?"

"I have no classes on Fridays. We can start this Friday if you want."

"That's perfect, what time on Friday?"

"What time is good for you?" She asked.

"Sometime in the afternoon, around 1pm?"

"That works! See you then," she said as she got up and was getting ready to leave.

"See you then," Zach said as he exited the classroom right after her.

Rain's next class was psychology. She thought this class would be interesting. She was fascinated with the study of the human brain. The professor went over the syllabus and what was required reading for the designated assignments. After he explained all that was required, he dismissed the class early.

After class ended, Rain decided to grab lunch at the cafeteria. Then she decided to head home. She got in her car, blasted k-love. On the way, she thought how great the day had gone. She loved her classes so far. She couldn't wait to tell her mom and dad about her first day back. She parked in the driveway on the other side of her mom's car. Her dad didn't mind parking his car on the street. She got out of her car and walked excitedly to the front door, she unlocked it and stepped inside. No one was downstairs, so she checked upstairs in her mom's room. Her mom was typing away at her laptop. She was working from home today. She stopped typing and looked up to see Rain in the doorway.

"Hey, Hon! How was your first day back?" she asked.

"Great! It was really great. I loved both classes today. They seem like they are going to challenge me, and that's a good thing," she added. "How is your day going?"

"Great. I'm just trying to finish up this report for my lawyer's client. Oh, there is food downstairs if you're hungry."

"I'm not hungry. I just ate the cafeteria. I'm going to go to my room and relax for a little. I'll leave you to finish up what you are doing," Rain said.

"Ok, yes. I must finish this, but I'm glad you had a great day back," she added.

Rain left her mom's room, closing the door behind her. Her room was next to her the office. She often wondered why her mom never chose to work in the office, but she guessed she just liked working in her room better.

Rain walked past the office and went to her room. In her sanctuary, as she liked to call it, she sat on her bed and looked around the room. She loved just looking at her artwork splashed across her room. Each piece had a special meaning to it. She wrote what each piece meant in a separate journal from her normal writing journal. She would title the piece of art she created and write a description of what it meant.

One day, when her artwork is displayed in an art gallery, she could refer to the description in her journal to explain the pieces. After she surveyed the room, she decided to go over to her easel and finish the painting she started. The painting was of a dove in front of a cross, with scripture references all around it. After she finished the painting, she went to the bathroom to clean her brushes off. When the brushes were all clean, she laid them on a paper towel to dry. She went to check on her mother again. She cracked her mom's bedroom door to find her mom fast asleep on her bed. She decided not to wake her and went downstairs to grab something to eat.

In the kitchen, she found leftovers from the night before. She made a plate of food and heated it up in the microwave. After it was finished warming up, she sat down at the kitchen table to eat.

* * *

The first week of college flew by at the speed of light. Before Rain knew it, it was Friday. Even though Rain had no classes on Fridays, she agreed to meet her classmate Zach to work on the project for Intro to Abstract Art. The library was full of students studying, reading books, and using the computer for research. Rain entered the library at 1pm, and she surveyed the room looking for Zach, but he was nowhere to be found. She decided to wait by the front door of the library, so she sat on a couch. After a few minutes, she checked her cell for the time. It was 1:15pm. As soon as she looked up a blond-haired boy with jeans and a sweatshirt was standing in front of her. It was Zach.

"Sorry, I'm a little late. It was traffic. Lunchtime, you know," he apologized.

"It's okay. No problem. Let's get to work," she said.

They first went to a nearby computer to look up artists who painted abstract art. Although there were many abstract artists, they chose to write about Wassily Wassilyevich Kandinsky. He was the pioneer of expressionism (abstract art). The assignment was to research and write about the artist of their choice, and then they had to recreate one of the abstract paintings that they did.

Zach and Rain spent two hours researching and gathering notes to compile in a paper. They also chose what abstract art of Wassily Wassilyevich Kandinsky that would recreate. They wanted to recreate the painting of the Church of St. Ursula. So, for the next two Fridays, they chose to meet at the same time of 1pm to do more research. Then one Friday, everything changed.

3

RESEARCH GONE WRONG

This particular Friday, Zach told Rain he has something to do at 1pm. He asked if they could meet at 7pm in the small room of the art building. She agreed to meet him around then. They had finished the writing portion of the project, so all they had to finish was the recreation of the Church of St. Ursula painting.

They met each other in the library before walking to the art building. The art building was adjacent to the library, so it wasn't a far walk to get there. Once in the art building, they found an open room to work in. In this room, there were different paintings displayed. They looked around the room at all the paintings, and after that, they grabbed a large piece of canvas. Rain started to outline the drawing from a picture on her phone.

"That's awesome!" Zach praised her.

"Thank you," she gushed. "Will you get the colors we need to paint the drawing?"

"Sure, let me see the painting again, so I know what colors to choose."

She showed him the photo of the painting on her cell.

He looked intently at the painting, and then went over to the paint station to find the colors that they needed to paint with.

"Here's purple, green, yellow, red, orange, blue," he said as he put them on the table one by one, as Rain continued to outline the painting. After ten minutes, Rain was all done outlining. They had all the colors laid out before them, and the picture of the painting was up on her cell phone. They each grabbed a brush and started painting in the outline.

Zach started with green, and Rain started with blue. They continued as the painting was taking shape.

"Hey Rain, how about showing me how to mix colors together?"

"How about we finish the painting first, then I will give you a quick lesson," she explained.

"God, you are so beautiful. I'm just noticing now. Spending this past couple of Fridays together getting to know you was awesome."

"Why thank you, but let's focus on the project. We still have a lot of painting to do," she said as she tried to deter him, but he continued.

"Where is the weirdest place you ever had sex?"

"Umm...let's get back to the painting Zach," she said, ignoring his previous eerie question.

"No, really, I want to know," he said as he placed his hand on her shoulder.

"Umm...Zach please, we have to get back to the painting," she told him again.

He slowly wrapped his arms around her waist and turned her towards him. She was beginning to feel frightened, and she knew it must have shown on her face.

"God, you are so beautiful," he repeated, this time whispering in her ear.

"Zach...please. The painting..." she tried to push away as her voice started to shake. He didn't let her move though, and he pulled her even closer.

* * *

After it was all said and done, he got up from on top of her and buttoned his jeans back up. Rain was left lying there, in shock at what had just happened. After he left, Rain started to cry uncontrollably. She then slowly got up and fixed her clothes. She spotted a night custodian but wanted to dodge him, so she ducked back down so he couldn't see her.

As soon as he was out of sight, she ran out of the art building to her car. She sat in her car for a long time pondering what just happen to her. She started her car engine and drove in silence to her house.

Upon approaching the front door to unlocked it, she looked through the window to see if her parents were still awake. They weren't. The coast was clear. She opened the front door and went straight to her room.

In her room, she ripped all her paintings down. She couldn't stand the paintings anymore, not after tonight. She started to shake uncontrollably. She went to the bathroom, and there was blood. She looked in the mirror, and she didn't see herself. She lifted up her shirt and found bruises were blossoming everywhere on her body. She just collapsed on the bathroom floor, crying. She cried for 20 minutes straight before she opted not to take a shower. She felt dirty, but she couldn't stand to see her naked body as it was just violated. After she left the bathroom, she climbed into her bed and fell asleep.

* * *

The next morning, Rain woke up at 10 am. She never slept past 7 am, even on the weekends, but her body went through a traumatic experience last night. It needed to heal itself. She decided to take a shower. In the shower, she scrubbed all over her body. She scrubbed so hard it made her bruises more noticeable even on her brown skin. After the shower, she just threw on some sweats and sneakers. She didn't even manage to tame her curly fro. After she got dressed, she went downstairs, praying her parents decided to sleep in. She was wrong, both of them were in the kitchen eating the big breakfast her mom cooks on the weekends.

"Honey?" her mom said. "I went to check on you to see if you wanted breakfast, but you were still sleeping. Are you okay? You don't look so good."

"I'm fine, mom. I just had a rough night last night," she said.

"How about some breakfast. It will make you feel better," she added.

"Umm...okay." Rain sat down to the plate her mom fixed and ate in silence.

"So honey, how's your art project going?" her dad asked.

"Fine, we ummm...yeah it's going fine," she told him.

"Well, that's great. I know you will ace this project," he added proudly.

Rain gave him a half-smile and continued to eat.

"Honey, are you sure you're okay? You don't seem like yourself today?" Her mom questioned her.

"I'm fine, mom. Really, I'm fine," she said, lying.

"Okay, I'm just checking," her mom said reassuringly.

"Mom, dad, can I be excused?" she asked.

"Of course, honey," her dad answered.

Rain excused herself from the table because she didn't want to keep faking that she was okay when she felt like a numb zombie inside. *She had to tell someone about what happened to her. She couldn't keep this secret forever. Did she lead him on? She wondered. Was she too playful in her mannerisms to make him believe she wanted to have sex with him?* All these thoughts ran through her mind. She never thought she would associate the word rape as something she would be a victim of. She still couldn't believe it happened to her.

The next week after her assault was a living hell for her. She experienced the worse panic attacks. She would have flashbacks throughout the day, which would get more intense at night to where she would wake up screaming. She stopped painting, drawing, and writing during this time because she couldn't bring herself to be creative, even though that may have helped her cope during the aftermath. She continued to lie to her parents about what really happened to her that night because she felt ashamed and felt like it was her fault.

* * *

Even a month after the assault, things were no different in regards to how she felt. Her panic attacks got increasingly worse, and her flashbacks more intense. She didn't know how much longer she could deal with this on her own. She skipped a lot of school during this time because she couldn't be in the same room as Zachary. She made excuses to her parents and professors as to why she wasn't there. She had to talk to someone before she lost her mind trying to cope on her own. She searched on her tablet about how women dealt with the aftermath of a sexual assault because she didn't know what to do. There were a lot of resources that dealt with this, and she was overwhelmed at the number of women that deal with this type of trauma. She decided to make an appointment with a rape crisis counselor because she couldn't keep lying to her parents and living this hellish nightmare that was eating away at her core every single day.

She called a local center and spoke to the secretary. The secretary asked her if it was her first time coming to a center like this and told her that name of the counselor that she would be setting her appointment with, Dr. Adams. The secretary made the appointment for the next day since she could hear in Rain's voice how troubled she was since she wasn't able to collect her thoughts while she was speaking to her. The secretary told her, "You will meet with Dr. Adams tomorrow morning at 10 am. She will be expecting you. I don't want you to have to keep coping with this on your own."

* * *

Rain barely slept the through the night after she spoke with the secretary. She was nervous about the appointment, plus she still was having nightmares and flashbacks. She told her parents that she was going to an appointment this morning, but she didn't disclose what type of appointment it was.

On the drive to the center, she couldn't believe she was about to explain to someone what happened to her a month before. A whole month had passed since that horrific night, the memory still so fresh in her mind like it happened yesterday. She couldn't think too long about it, or she would have a panic attack while driving. She turned on the radio to ease her mind.

Once she arrived at the center, she walked inside to a little office that was filled with posters and pamphlets about all the different types of programs and groups that helped women dealing with this type of trauma. She went up to the front desk, where there was a sign-in sheet. Rain signed her name, the time, date, and the name of the counselor she would be speaking with. After she signed in, she took a seat and waited for her name to be called. There were a few people in front of her on the list, but it only took about fifteen minutes for her name to be called.

"Rain Thompson, the secretary called. Dr. Adams is expecting you. I'm so glad you decided to come," she added.

"I will show you to her office."

The secretary walked Rain past a few offices before stopping at Dr. Adams's office. As soon as she stopped at her office, the secretary went inside, came back out, and motioned to Rain that she could go into her office now.

"Hi. You must be Rain. I'm Dr. Adams. I will be talking with you today. My secretary was so concerned when you called to make an appointment that she told me to fit you in this morning.

"Sexual assault is not an easy thing to categorized in regards to how an individual feels. People can feel a gamut of emotions, from blaming themselves to anger to depression. So, I'm glad you stopped in today to talk with me. How are you feeling?" she asked.

"I feel like I'm a walking zombie. I don't have any motivation. All I want to do is sleep, and that's not easy with rest being far, few, and in between. I wake up screaming in the middle of the night, have panic attacks, and flashbacks of that night. I haven't been to school for fear I would run into him. I have to continuously lie to everyone about how I'm feeling. It's taking a toll on me and my sanity," Rain explained.

"Do you mind me asking, when did this happen?"

"A month ago. It's been a whole month of hell of earth. I literally thought I was going to lose my mind dealing with the aftermath of this. I never knew that this is what it feels likes to experience something so traumatic," Rain answered.

"Here's what I'm going to do, I'm going to give you samples of meds to help with your anxiety, PTSD, and the flashbacks. I'm going to recommend a women's support group in the area for you to attend. It is located at the recreational building. You should see signs up, once you get there.

The group leader is named Layla. She has a group of roughly 10 or so women that have been through what you've been through. I think it would be helpful to you to see how other women cope, to have support on this road to healing. I think the next meeting is on Sunday at 12 noon if you can stop by to introduce yourself and hear what the group entails that would be wonderful. Is that something you would be interested in?" she asked

"Yes, I would be interested in attending this group. Do I have to do anything, or can I just show up?" Rain questioned.

"You don't have to do anything. It's free and open to all women. All you have to do is show up," Dr. Adams stated.

"Here are some sample meds I was telling you about. Take one in the morning and one at night. If you have any side effects or the meds make you feel worse, call me immediately, okay? And I hope you can attend the meeting this Sunday. I really think it will help," she added

Rain reassured her that she would try to attend the meeting and take the meds like she prescribed. She wanted to heal and find effective coping mechanisms to help her deal with what she'd been experiencing as of late.

4

CONFESSIONS OF A TORTURED ARTIST

Rain had to lie, yet again to her parents so she could skip church to attend the meeting her counselor told her about at the local recreational building. When she walked into the room, she saw empty chairs that formed a circle and a podium with a mic attached to it. She was the first one there, so she walked around looking at the pamphlets they had on display. One of the pamphlets caught her eye. It was a pamphlet telling about the services they had in a psychiatric ward to help victims of rape. She took one of the pamphlets to read up on later.

Soon women started filling in, women her age, middle-aged women, and senior age women. She couldn't believe the spectrum of women who had gone through the same traumatic experience. She decided to sit down in a chair and wait for the speaker to come up. Everyone finally sat down and were talking among themselves. Rain sat quietly. She just wanted to observe the surroundings and take in the moment.

The group leader approached the podium and introduced herself to the women. Layla, who appeared to be in her mid-30's, had long blonde hair and green eyes. She was wearing a long skirt with a floral print on it and a shirt that matched the purple in one of the flowers. She continued to explain why she started the group. The idea came ten years ago when she visited a group similar to this one when she was sexually assaulted by her then boyfriend at the age of 20, in which she conceived a child. Her son Jonathan, aged ten, was home with her husband, Luke. She said that they had gone fishing on the lake today. She explained more of her journey as a rape survivor, that it wasn't easy, and told the women that they would get through this. She told them it wouldn't happen overnight, and it might even be a long process, but she promised them they would heal. She ended her speech by saying that her husband Luke accepted her son as his own, loved her, and was a critical piece to her healing.

Layla then opened up the floor by asking if there was anyone new to the group. A few women raised their hands, including Rain. Layla then proceeded to welcome them, and she asked if they would like to share at the podium. She told them that if not, they could listen to the other women who had been coming for a while share how far they've come since their assault happened. She also added that there would be light refreshments and a gathering afterward.

One by one, each woman came up to the podium to share their stories. Each of the stories were unique to their situations, but they were equally traumatizing. Rain decided to listen to the stories and take it all in. She wasn't quite ready to share her story with the group yet, possibly with Layla, but not with the entire group. After the last woman spoke, Layla came back up to the podium to introduce Heather, one of the staff members who worked at a local psychiatric ward. Heather went on to explain the types of programs and help that was geared towards rape victims. She explained that checking yourself voluntarily into a psych ward for a few weeks to get the help and support that they needed didn't mean you were crazy, but rather it meant that you care enough about your healing and wholeness. She mentioned her favorite quote that sums up the path to healing "Even though your wounds are not your fault, your healing is still your responsibility." This quote stuck with Rain. She wanted to heal from this. She wanted to be proactive in her healing process.

After the meeting, the women got up to go to the refreshment table. Each table was set up with cookies, cakes, pasta, meatballs, and a variety of drinks. Rain went over to the table to fix herself a plate. As she was doing so, Layla came over to her.

"Hi, I'm Layla. I saw you raise your hand when I asked if there were any new faces in the group. How did you enjoy the group?"

"Hi, my name is Rain. I really enjoyed the group and hearing the other stories on how these women overcame their sexual assault. I was assaulted a month ago by my classmate at college," she said after a pause.

Layla gave Rain a huge hug that lasted what seemed like forever. As they embraced, tears flowed from Rain's eyes.

Layla whispered to her, "It's okay. It's wasn't your fault.

You are loved in spite of what you went through. Don't let anyone tell you that you aren't lovable and that no one would love you because you experienced this. That's a lie. You are loved," she repeated.

After their embrace, Layla continued to ask Rain questions to get to know her and her story. Rain asked if that staff member from the psych ward that gave that presentation was still here because she wanted to speak with her. Layla told Rain that Heather was still here, and she would find her. Layla left Rain to go look for Heather, who was talking with a group of four women across the room. Rain watched as Layla motioned to Heather, pointing Rain out to her. Rain saw Heather nod her head and mouthed something back to Layla. Soon after the brief exchange with Heather, Layla made her way back over to Rain.

"As soon as she finishes talking to those women, she will come to find you, okay? Layla explained. "Do you want more food while you wait? Again, I'm so glad you came, Rain. I hope you continue to come and share your story with the group," she added.

"Thank you for having me. I plan to come again and build up the courage to share my story one of these days," she said.

Layla proceeded to hug Rain again and told her she had to go to check on her husband and son. She reminded her Heather should be with her shortly and told her to have a great day.

Heather walked up as soon as Layla left, she had naturally red hair, blue eyes, and was dressed in her scrubs.

"Hi, you must be Rain. You wanted to talk to me?"

"Yes, I have some questions about the programs in the psych ward regarding how they help sexual assault victims."

"Why, yes. Our facility using a wide variety of programs to assist in the healing process of sexual assault survivors. We have counseling sessions, art therapy, music therapy, yoga classes. Although there are people in the facility that haven't been sexual assaulted or abused, but they have other issues that they could be dealing with while they take these classes as well."

Rain listened intently as she explained the types of programs, how to be admitted into the facility, and other pertinent information about the facility. After Heather finished telling her about the facility, she asked Rain if she had any more questions.

"Can I give you my name and number so you can call me? I would be very interested in being admitted voluntarily," Rain informed her.

"Sure," Heather said. "I can take down your information and set you up to be admitted as soon as you want to. I can have a chat with Nurse Jones, the Nurse practitioner as soon as I leave here. I will get back to you in 48 hours, sound good?" Heather explained.

"Sounds good," Rain said. "It was nice meeting you. I look forward to speaking to you in two days."

"It was nice meeting you, Rain. I will keep in touch. Have a great day," Heather said as she left to go back to the facility.

Rain checked the time on her cell. It read 2pm. She was there for two hours; it was definitely time for her to leave. She didn't want her parents questioning her whereabouts because she was gone too long. She left the recreation building, got in her car, and drove straight home.

When she arrived home, she waited in her car for a few seconds just to rehearse what she was going to tell her parents who were most definitely going to ask her about why she was gone so long. But her conscious was telling her to tell the truth. Although she just confessed what happened to a total stranger, that seemed easier than making the confession to her own parents. She took a deep breath, before exhaling and made the decision that she would tell her parents what happened a month ago. She got out her car and walked to the front door, unlocked it, and stepping inside.

"Honey, where were you? I tried calling to check on you, but your phone went to voicemail," her mom said.

"Mom, I have to tell you something that happened to me a month ago."

A month ago, why are you deciding to tell me now? Why didn't you tell me when it happened?" she asked.

"Because I had to build up the courage to tell you. Remember the night, I went with Zach to work on our art project? Well, that's not all that happened that night. I'm still coming to grips with what happened. This is extremely hard for me say," Rain confessed

"Whatever is it, you can tell me. You don't have to be embarrassed," her mom said reassuringly.

"I was raped. Zach raped me," she finally blurted out.

"What? He did what?" She was in shock and couldn't believe what her daughter just told her.

"Yes, mom. I'm sorry I lied to you and dad about this

afternoon, but I was at a support meeting with sexual assault survivors," Rain explained.

Her mom grabbed her and hugged her tightly. She kept saying "My poor baby" over and over as she stroked her hair.

"Don't tell dad yet," Rain said. "He'll want to kill him."

"I won't honey, but soon he'll have to know," her mom said.

"I got some information about programs that they have in a local Psychiatric Ward for sexual assault survivors. I gave my name to the staff member who told me about this. I'm thinking of committing myself voluntarily," she added.

"Oh honey, I don't understand what you are going through, but why commit yourself when there are groups like that group you went to today. Why don't you just keep going there?" she asked.

"Because I need to get away. I haven't been going to school as it is because I don't want to have to face Zach. I don't want to have to go into the art building and remind myself that this was the place it happened," she said, tearing up again.

"Oh honey, if you have to go and commit yourself, I will back you 100%. You would have to take another leave of absence from college, and you just got back," she reminded her.

"At this point, I don't care. I will graduate when I'm supposed to graduate."

Rain had just remembered that she had the pamphlet from the meeting. So instead of waiting for Heather to call her back, she decided to call herself and set a date to be admitted into the psych ward.

5

POSTER CHILD: WOUNDS, HEALING & RESPONSIBILITY

Chase grew up too fast. He had no choice. Innocence was taken from him at a young age, and he was forced to deal with the memories of what no child should have to deal with.

His mother, Dana, and father, Ethan, married in their early 20's. They were high school sweethearts. They went to their senior prom together, and that's the night Chase was conceived. They both were graduating high school that same year, and they had come to a mutual agreement to co-parent Chase until Ethan was finished with college.

After Ethan graduated from college, Dana and he got married. Chase was then four years old. His mother worked in a local flower shop, while his father planned to open his art gallery 'Stroke of the Brush.' Soon after the art gallery opened, Chase's mother came on board as co-owner. Being around other artists, Chase gravitated to the arts as well. Chase had a pretty normal childhood from the ages of four to ten. After hitting his teenage years, everything went downhill.

His dad started coming home drunk and high all the time. It was the artists he was hanging around with who had art displayed in his gallery. At first, it's seemed like no big deal, but it started happening more frequently. Dana, Chase's mom, noticed a change in her husband's behavior and told him to seek help. He agreed to and spent several months in rehab.

When he was released and got home, that's when the problems got even worse. He took his anger out on Chase, who was now thirteen. His father blamed Chase for having him sent to rehab, even though it was Dana who suggested he go.

The physical abuse continued until he was fifteen years old.

Chase's mom had no clue that this was happening to her son. One day, Chase sat her down to explain to her what his dad was doing to him.

"Mom, can I talk to you for a minute?" he said

""Sure, what's on your mind?" Chase, his mom asked.

"It's about dad," he stated.

"What about your father?"

"Do you know Dad will beat me every time you're gone from the house. He gets so drunk, and he takes his anger out on me. Have you noticed the bruises on me, mom? You ever wondered where I got them from?" he asked.

"I did notice bruises on you, but I thought they were just from you being a kid, playing roughly with your friends," she explained. "Your dad kept telling me that you were very rough with your friends when you guys played."

"You never questioned him about it? You just took his word for it?"

"Why would I question him, he did get help. I don't know what you have against him, Chase. He would never hurt you. He loves you so much," she added.

"That's what you think. You are always taking his side, why? Don't you even care what I've been through?" he lashed out at her.

"Chase, I do care about you, but I really feel you are overacting. He's gotten help. He's changed, and if you can't see it, I can't help you see it," she explained.

Since his mother didn't believe him and he didn't want to be subjected to the abuse anymore, he went to live with his mom's sister in California.

* * *

His aunt welcomed him with open arms. Upon his arrival in California, he felt a peace and a release mentally from the haunting memories of the last few years. Chase's aunt Sarah helped him enroll in high school and was there to listen to any concerns he had.

The first few months of high school was an adjustment for Chase. He had to get used to his new teachers and his classmates. As soon as he was making good grades, excelling in his academics and arts, he got involved with the wrong crowd. He started skipping school, drinking, and doing drugs.

As a result of the excessive drinking and drug use, as well as past abuse, he developed PTSD. He started to have flashbacks of the abuse he suffered at the hands of his father. These flashbacks were so intense, he began to cut himself to ease the pain.

His Aunt Sarah was starting to notice his changing behavior. He could only hide it for so long. One day, she sat Chase down to have a chat with him.

"Chase, what's going on? You've not been yourself for the past couple of weeks," his aunt said as concern weaved across her face.

"I'm just a little stressed with school, but everything is fine," Chase said, clearly lying. "I'm just a little tired right now. Can I be excused to my room?" he added.

"Of course, but if you want or need to talk, I'm here. You know I love you," she said reassuringly.

"Yes, I know, and I love you too, Auntie."

He got up, hugged her, kissed her forehead, and went to his room. In his room, he blasted his music so loud the whole house shook. He thought to himself, *I have to do something tonight. She is on to me.* He went into his bookbag, where he stashed the pills his friends gave him to relax his mind, and he took eight of them after that he got the bottle of vodka he kept under his bed and drank the whole thing. He collapsed on his bedroom floor.

Sarah was downstairs and heard the music blasting. A few times, she yelled, "Chase, turn down that music." But after a while of no change in the music's volume, she decided to check on him. *Maybe he can't hear me yelling,* she thought. On her way to Chase's room, she smelled vodka seeping out from under the door. She quickly opened his door. "Chase, I told you..." her voice trailed off as she rushed to grab her cell and call 911. Chase was lying on the floor unresponsive.

She started CPR and mouth to mouth until the ambulance arrived and transported Chase to the hospital. At the hospital, she nervously waited for Chase to wake up. She was questioned by the nurses and doctors and filled out tons of paperwork. The verdict was that Chase had to go to rehab, A.A, as well as counseling.

Upon his release from the hospital, Chase had to sign paperwork saying he would commit to the programs and do the necessary homework required. Failing to do so would result in termination and the inability to go back for six months. He understood the severity of his situation and promised his aunt Sarah that he would do as the doctors told. His aunt even offered to accompany him to his counseling sessions, but Chase told her he would be fine to go to the sessions alone.

Post hospitalization, it was time for Chase's first counseling session. Sarah had to sacrifice time away from work to take him to his sessions and meetings.

It was the first counseling session with Dr. Calum. As soon as they pulled up to his office, Sarah asked Chase one more time if he would like her to accompany him at least for the first few sessions. He said no. That he would be able to handle this alone. She respected his wishes and said she would pick him up in an hour.

Chase entered the building and went to the front desk to sign in. The secretary was surprisingly nice. She gave Chase yet more paperwork to fill out and a confidentiality agreement to sign. After filling out the paperwork, he took a seat to wait until the therapist was ready to see him. While he waited, he skimmed through an art magazine they had on display.

"Chase," the secretary called, "Dr. Calum, will see you now."

Chase didn't know what to expect from the session, but he was going with an open mind. He entered Dr. Calum's office, and he noticed all the psych books on the Doctor's shelf and a huge poster saying "Your wound is probably not your fault, but your healing is your responsibility." That saying hit Chase at his core. He knew he couldn't play the blame game anymore. In fact, getting to the point where he didn't want to place blame would take a lot of work, but that's why he was here, right?

Dr. Calum was a man around his mid 50's. He had salt and pepper hair and wore black glasses. He greeted Chase and motioned him to take a seat.

"So, what brings you to my office this afternoon?" Dr. Calum asked as he thumbed through the paperwork Chase filled out while he was in the waiting room.

"Well, a lot of things I'm dealing with and have yet to work through."

"I see. Well, let's start with your family history. How was

your childhood growing up? It states here that your aunt is your primary caregiver. Did you grow up with her?" he inquired.

"No, I didn't grow up with her. I came to live with her a few months ago after my home life went downhill," Chase stated.

"What happened at home that made you want to live with your aunt?" Dr. C asked, trying to dig deep so Chase would open up.

Chase tried to look down, but he was met with Dr. C's reassuring glance. "Take your time, Chase. We have many sessions together. You don't have to tell me all at once," he assured Chase.

"Well, my childhood from age four to about ten was pretty normal. I lived with my mom and dad. My mom worked at a flower shop until my dad opened his art gallery, and then she came on board to help him."

"It seemed like to me you had a great childhood. What happened after age ten?"

Chase took a deep breath. He never talked about his abuse to anyone before, except to his mom and aunt. He didn't want to be judged or told it was his fault like his mother told him.

"This is a safe place. Nothing is discussed outside this office," Dr. C explained to him.

Chase finally mustered up the courage to tell him. "My father started coming home high and drunk all the time, and he took his anger out on me."

"How so? Did he hit you?"

Chase nodded. "Yes," he said as his voice got softer.

He took an even bigger deep breathe, before speaking. Looking down to the floor, Chase said, "No one believed me. Not even my own mother."

"I believe you. I wouldn't doubt anything you tell me. It's not my job to take sides. It's my job to listen and get you the necessary help," he said reassuringly. "Have you spoken to your parents about how you feel?"

"No, I haven't spoken to either of them since I came to live with my aunt. I'm not ready to confront them yet," Chase explained.

"You know, you can't keep how you are feeling inside forever. It's not healthy. You're going to have to speak to them, clear the air, and try to heal," Dr. C. said matter of factly.

"I know, but it has to be on my own terms, and frankly, I'm just not ready to face them head-on right now," Chase stated.

"Well, you will when you are ready. I'm sorry, but our time is up today. We'll finish talking about this in the next session if that's okay?"

"Sure. Thanks for listening to me, Dr. C. I appreciate it," Chase said as he got up to shake Dr. C's hand.

"No problem. See you next time. Have a great rest of your day," Dr. C said as he led him to the door.

Chase left the session feeling lighter. That was the first time he ever discussed what happened to him. Even though it was the hardest thing he'd ever done, he felt a release once he spoke about it.

Chase called his aunt to see where she was. She told him that she was fifteen minutes away and that she stopped to get food for them to eat. Chase told her that he would be waiting outside, sitting on a nearby bench in front of the office.

Aunt Sarah pulled up in her black Honda Accord. Chase opened the passenger door, sat down, and put his seat-belt on. The car smelled of Chinese food. He was so hungry that he wondered what she got.

"So, how was the first session?" Sarah asked.

"It was good. I talked about things that I held inside for the longest. It's felt good to speak to someone about it," he told her.

"I'm glad to hear that Chase. I bought you sesame chicken with white rice from the Chinese place."

"Yum! I'm starving. I haven't eaten since breakfast."

Soon, they were back to Sarah's house, and she unlocked the door. They entered and both when to the living room. She put the Chinese food bag on the coffee table, and Chase dug through it and found his food. He then grabbed the plastic utensils, opened it up, and started to eat.

"I'm going to take a shower first, don't eat my food," she joked.

Aunt Sarah gave Chase the look of death as she went up the stairs to take her shower.

Chase continued to eat. After he was finished, he cleaned up his plate and went to his room. In his room, he picked up his notebook filled with drawings, writings, and other randomness. He started to draw his feelings about the session with Dr. C today. He used a lot of light colors to represent his newfound clarity and peace of mind he gained talking with him. It was the first time in a long time that he used lighter colors. All his other drawings were dark and depressing and used a lot of red and black. He was kind of relieved, but in the back of his mind, he wondered if feelings of anger, hurt, and pain would resurface again.

6

RELIVING RELAPSE

Everything was fine for the next few years. Chase was compliant with going to his A.A meetings and counseling sessions, and even Dr. Calum noticed his tremendous progress. But that progress would soon be short-lived as Chase started to fall back in with the same group of friends that landed him in the hospital the first time.

One day after high school, Chase came home very drunk and high. He had gone to his friend's house where they just sat around drinking and getting high. Chase stumbled home and went straight to his room. Aunt Sarah wasn't home from work yet, so it was easy enough for him to sober up before she got there. He didn't sober up quick enough to deal with the tormenting thoughts that haunted him from his past.

He went downstairs in the kitchen to grab the sharpest knife there was. He was going to put a stop to the thoughts that haunted him since he was thirteen years old. He finally found a knife he thought would do the job. He held out both arms and begun cutting himself. Blood splattered everywhere in the kitchen, and it looked like a murder scene.

Aunt Sarah pulled up to the driveway and got out of her car. She preceded to open the front door, and that's when she saw Chase lying in a pool of blood.

"Chase!" she screamed. She dialed 911 immediately.

The ambulance came quickly, and Chase had to be given a blood transfusion in route to the hospital. His aunt Sarah was so scared that she might have lost him, but she was very grateful that the ambulance got there as soon as they could.

At the hospital, Sarah had to fill out more paperwork just like the first time she went through this with him. She couldn't figure out how to help him. She thought the counseling and A.A meetings were helping because she had been given good reports about Chase's progress, but she wondered what happened.

The doctor finally came out to the waiting room and told Sarah that Chase was stabilized and that she could go see him. She walked into his hospital room slowly. She didn't know what to say to him. She couldn't believe that she was in the same place that she was a few years ago with him.

"Chase, how are you feeling?" Sarah asked.

"Ummm...I'm okay. I'm sorry I put you through this again," he said softly.

"I can't keep doing this. It's taking a toll on me. You are going to have to get help," she pleaded.

"It didn't help. I refuse to go back to the sessions and meetings. I'd rather deal with it on my own," he stated.

"I'm sorry. I can't have you stay with me. I can't do this

anymore. It's too taxing on me. You are going to have to go back to your mom and dad's," she explained.

"What??? You wouldn't dare send me back to live with them," he said, shocked.

"I have no choice. You won't go back to counseling or A.A. What am I supposed to do? Watch you kill yourself? I won't do that Chase," she said.

"So, what now? Are you going to call my parents?" Chase asked.

"I've already spoken to them. They are waiting for you to come back. They really want you to come back because they miss you," she answered. "Maybe it will be different."

"I can't believe... different, different..." his voice trailed off.

"I'm sorry. It just has to be this way," she explained.

He just turned away from her and didn't say anything more. She then proceeded to get up and exit his room, leaving him alone.

They kept him in the hospital for a few more days to monitor him. After his release, his aunt Sarah decided to allow Chase to stay for two weeks to get a chance to heal fully. After the two weeks were up, he would be sent back to live with his parents. Chase was grateful for the two weeks to stay with his aunt before going home, but he was still upset about the fact that he had to go back.

The first week back at his aunt's house, Chase spent his time packing his belongings to bring back to his parents' house. He also went to say goodbye to his classmates, friends, and teachers. It was very bittersweet. All his classmates and teachers had good things to say about him and gave him some parting gifts to bring home with him.

Sarah picked him up from school that day, and Chase was so grateful for all the gifts everyone gave him. He couldn't wait to show Sarah. She wasn't shocked that everyone was fond of Chase, even despite what he had gone through these few past years, he was a very caring, smart, and loving person.

"Look! Look what my teachers, classmates, and friends gave me," he said. He was carrying bags full of goodies, like gift cards, candy, and letters.

"Awesome! I know you are going to miss them all," Sarah said lovingly.

"Yes, I am, going to miss them," he said somberly. "And I'm going to miss you to auntie."

"I'm going to miss you too, but I know this is part of the healing process for you. You can't run from the past forever."

"I know, and I was very upset with you when you told me I had to go back to live with my parents, but I need to confront them and tell them how I've been feeling."

"Yes, you do. I have a surprise for you before you head back home next week," she said excitedly.

"You do?" he asked.

"I know how you love to draw, so I booked an artist retreat where you can spend this weekend learning more about your craft," she stated.

"Oh, wow, thanks auntie," he said.

"You're welcome, hon. You know I love you."

"I love you too."

* * *

It was the first day the Artist Retreat. The retreat was at a local university. Chase has packed his bags to stay in one of the dorms for Friday, Saturday, and Sunday. He was very excited to learn more about his craft and meet with other artists. As soon as he got to the university, there was a sign that said "Artist Retreat: Painting Your Passion" located in the Fine Arts building 248. So, his aunt drove around the university looking for building 248, once she found it, she parked her car and let Chase out.

"Have a great time Chase and call me on Sunday and let me know what time to pick you up," she stated.

"Will do. Thanks again for giving me this opportunity, see you Sunday," he answered and turned to walk up the steps into the building.

Once in the building, there was a registration table with the attendees' names, room numbers, and roommates. He greeted the woman at the table and said his name. She then gave him a bag with the schedule of events, name tag, room number, and roommate's name. She mentioned that there would be a welcome meeting at 10 am, where they would explain where everything was going to be held. There he would meet who he was to room with.

Chase looked around as people started to file into the building towards the registration table. There were all types of people: young, middle-aged, and older adults. They were all coming together in the name of art. He decided to head towards to conference room where they were going to have the welcome meeting. He entered the room and took a seat somewhere between the middle and back of the room. He sat down and started to look at the schedule of workshops and events for this weekend. They had a beginning, intermediate, and advanced drawing and painting classes. They had lectures on how to market and sell your drawings and paintings. Finally, for entrepreneurs, a business class if you wanted to start your own art gallery.

People started to come into the conference room for the welcome meeting. A guy who looked to be in his mid-twenties who was wearing a button-down shirt and khaki pants came and sat next to Chase.

"Hi, my name is Shane. What's your name?" the gentleman asked.

"My name is Chase. Nice to meet you, Shane. What brings you here?"

"I'm a businessman, who loves artistic pieces, and I would like to open my own art gallery one day," Shane explained. "How about you?"

"Well, this retreat was a going away gift from my aunt. I draw and paint as a hobby, and I just want to connect with other artists, like myself," Chase said.

"Oh, I see, not from here? Where are you from? You said a going away gift?" Shane asked.

"I'm not from California. I'm from Pennsylvania, and I just came to live with my aunt a few years ago," he stated.

"Oh, how you liking California? I love it here, born and raised."

"It took a lot getting used to the fast pace, but I love it. I love the warm weather every single day. That's something I've gotten used to."

"You have a roommate for this weekend? I know they assigned us one, but since we just are getting to know one another, want to room together this weekend?" Shane asked.

"Sure, of course. We can room together.," Chase said.

As soon as Chase said that, the retreat speaker came on stage to welcome all the attendees and explain the weekend workshops and classes. He also mentioned there was a table outside where, if you were staying on the campus, you could see who you were rooming with. Chase and Shane went to the table and requested a change regarding roommates. After swapping, they headed to the dorm rooms.

Shane being the businessman that he was, brought a suitcase and Chase brought a duffel bag. They each got their respective belongings and started making their way to the dorms. Once in the dorms, the event committee had a certain number of dorms for the attendees. So, Shane and Chase picked the first empty dorm room. They surveyed the room, chose their beds, and put belongings down.

"Workshops, start tomorrow, according to the schedule," Shane said. "They have a welcome lunch at noon, where we can meet the other attendees and instructors. Would you like to go?"

"Sure, I'm starving, and it would be great to meet other people too."

"All right, let me just call my girlfriend and tell her I made it to the retreat safely."

"Hey, Lindsey, I made it here safely. The people are cool, and the classes start tomorrow. Yes, my roommate is cool, from Pennsylvania. All right, honey, I will talk to you later, love you. Bye," he said as he proceeded to hang up the phone. "Sorry, I wanted to let her know I was here..."

"No, problem," Chase answered. "Are you ready to go down to the luncheon?"

"Yeah, let's go," Shane replied.

Shane and Chase left their bag and suitcase on their respective beds, locked the door to their dorm room, and headed to the dining hall. In the dining hall, they had all types of food, American, Indian, Greek, Italian, etc., and a massive amount of desserts from cakes, cookies, and cupcakes. It was like they'd stepped into food heaven. They both looked at each other, wondering where to start. Chase went to the Indian food, but Shane wasn't that bold enough to venture from the American food. After they got their food, they found a semi-empty table to sit at.

They both sat down and said hello to the two ladies and one gentleman that were already seated and eating their food. The two ladies were in their early 30s, were friends that came together. They both were professional artists and were at the retreat to hone their craft. The gentleman in his early 40s, an art teacher who wanted to get new ideas to teach his classes. It was truly a mixture of all ages, backgrounds, and professions.

After they ate, Chase and Shane went to the art display room, it was filled with art from this year's workshop instructors and from last year attendees. Chase was very inspired by the different drawings and paintings displayed, and he couldn't wait to participate in the workshops in the morning.

The next morning, breakfast was at 8:30am, so both Chase and Shane got up and got dressed. Shane told Chase that he would meet him down at breakfast. He had to call his girlfriend first. So, Chase left for the dining hall.

Breakfast was the same regarding the amount and variety. *Food heaven times two*, Chase thought to himself. He ended up trying a variety of different breakfast foods, and he didn't want the standard American breakfast. He tried some Indian, Greek, Spanish, Italian breakfast foods. He loved trying new foods. After he ate, he looked to see if he saw Shane, because the workshops were about to start. But when he didn't, he decided to go ahead to the first workshop, which was an intermediate painting and drawing workshop.

In the workshop, they got to paint and draw abstract art, mix colors, and learn about the craft of art in a whole new way. Chase was very intrigued and inspired by the workshop instructors and the other attendees' drawings and paintings.

After the workshop was over, Chase went back to the dorm room to take a nap. Getting up at 8am for breakfast, and then the workshop made him tired. He needed a rest. He wondered where Shane was, because he hadn't seen him all day. But again, there were tons of workshops, so they could have bypassed each other. Chase laid on his bed and fell fast asleep.

Two hours later, he woke up to a voice talking on the phone. It was Shane again talking to his girlfriend, Lindsey. He laid there for a few more minutes to compose himself.

"Love you too, darling, see you tomorrow afternoon," Shane said to Lindsey hanging up his phone.

"Hey Chase, how was the workshop you went to?" he asked

"Oh, it was so inspiring. I learned a lot," he said excitedly. "How about you?"

"Very informative. I know how to make a business plan, market, and search for buildings for my art gallery," he said.

"Awesome," Chase added.

* * *

It was the final day of the Artist Retreat. Breakfast was continental on Sunday. Both Chase and Shane packed their things the night before. So, when they got up in the morning, they each got a shower and got dressed. They exchanged contact information before heading down to breakfast and the closing ceremony.

In the closing ceremony, awards were given out and art by this year, attendees were displayed in the lobby. A few of Chase's artwork and paintings were part of the displays, which made him very excited to know in this short weekend, he has grown as an artist.

Once the ceremony was over, he said his goodbyes to Shane, wished him luck in his endeavors, and told him to keep in touch. Chase then called his aunt Sarah to pick him up from the university, as soon as she could.

Twenty minutes later, Sarah was there eagerly awaiting Chase's reaction to the retreat. Sarah opened her trunk so Chase could put his duffel bag in. He came around after placing the bag in the trunk, opened the car door, and sat down.

"So...how was it?" Sarah asked.

"It was so inspiring. I loved it, and I met so many people. I learned about the art of art," he said with a smile.

"I'm so glad you love the retreat," she said, echoing his excitement.

"Yes, I did. Thank you, auntie, for allowing me this opportunity."

"You're welcome, love."

When they arrived home, Sarah ordered pizza while Chase went upstairs to continue packing for his trip back to Pennsylvania. He still wasn't too thrilled about moving back with his parents, but sooner or later he had to confront them. It had been years since he'd spoken to or seen either of them. He wanted to keep his distance because the pain was still too real for him.

The day finally came where he has to say goodbye to his Aunt Sarah. They both cried as they sat in her car in front of the airport.

"Call me when you land and when Dana picks you up, okay?" she told him.

"Okay, I will, auntie. Thanks so much for all you've done for me. I love you," he said.

"I love you too, Chase," she said as she let him out of her car. She gave him one final hug, and off into the distance, he walked. She watched him disappear into the airport.

7

THE JOURNEY HOME

Chase boarded the plane back to Pennsylvania. On the plane ride home, which was six hours, he had time to reflect. He reflected on his life in CA, the mistakes he made and the grief he caused his aunt. But he also reflected on the good times with his aunt and how he healed through therapy and the A.A meetings. But he was also frightened about what this next chapter in PA would be like. He had hardly spoken to his parents since being in CA, and in those three years, he had no desire to visit them. He just wanted to put the past behind him, but here he was getting ready to confront what he spent three years running from.

He finally landed in Pennsylvania. The first thing he did was call his aunt Sarah and told her he has just arrived in PA. His aunt was grateful to hear he arrived safely, told him that she would visit him shortly, and that she loved him. He told her he loved her and was grateful she let him stay with her for three years. After they finished speaking, they both hung up. Chase took a deep breath because the next person he had to call was his mother. He has not spoken to her, by choice, for three years, and now he was about to break that silent streak.

He dialed his mother's number, but his nerves were on edge as the phone rang, rang, rang. Then, he heard his mother's voice, "Chase? Chase, is that you?" she said softly.

"Yes, it's me. I'm back in PA, and I just landed. I need you to come pick me up from the airport," he explained.

"Sarah told me you'd be arriving sometime today; I just didn't know what time. I will be there in thirty minutes," she said.

"Ok, we'll talk when you get here," he said.

Chase hung up from talking with his mother thinking *what did I get myself into.* He had thirty minutes to agonize over how the conversation may go once he was sitting across from her in the car. He thought, maybe he would keep his headphones on and pretend he was listening to music. Maybe he would act sleepy and pretend to sleep. It's been three long years since speaking with his parents. Now having to think about the past and old feelings surfacing made him nauseous. The thought of seeing and being around his mother for the first time since she said he was lying about the abuse he suffered still stung to his core. But like his aunt Sarah told him before he left CA, he couldn't run from his past anymore. He needed to face his fears head on.

Soon he saw his mom's car. She got out, grabbed his suitcase, and his carry on. She then sat Chase's belongings inside the trunk and slammed it shut. After that, she proceeded to give Chase a long hug and which he reluctantly gave her.

"I missed you so much. The house wasn't the same without you," she stated

Chase didn't answer her. He just got in the car, and he put his seatbelt and headphones on. His mother started to drive to their house. The whole ride you could have heard a pin drop it was so silent. As soon as they got home, Chase got his suitcase and carry on out of the trunk and took it to his room.

His room was the same way he left it. Nothing had changed. His bed, furniture, and everything in his room was the same. He found his old journal/sketchbook and started to skim through it, but he had to stop because it was triggering bad thoughts and memories. No sooner than he put the book down, his mother called him for dinner.

"I'm coming," Chase yelled.

"It's your favorite! I made Chinese food."

Chase proceeded to go downstairs, and he could smell the aroma of sesame chicken, broccoli, and rice. He was starving and hadn't eaten since the meal they first gave him on the plane a few hours after take-off.

"Thanks, mom. It smells so good," he said, fixing his plate.

"My pleasure! And how are you doing? Days were hard around here without you. Your dad and I missed you. We got through. The gallery is going well, sold a couple of pieces, signed on a few new artists to display their work. Business is doing very well," she told him.

"That's great! I'm glad to hear the gallery is doing well. I'm okay, processing a lot right now, but I just need some time," he explained as he finished a piece of chicken.

"You haven't seen us in three years, so I understand it can be a little awkward. Take your time, just know if you need someone to talk to, I'm always here," she explained.

Chase continued to devour his food. As soon as he was finished, he got up and put his plate in the sink.

"I'm going for a drive," he stated. "I'll be back in a little while."

"Don't be too long! Your dad will be coming home in a few, and I'm sure he wants to see you," she explained.

Chase ignored the part his mother said about his dad. He thought to himself, *he's the last person I want to see.* After she said that he got up and just left.

He got in his father's old Black Mustang and started to drive. He had no point of destination. He just wanted to drive, listen to music, and clear his mind. He had a lot of time to think and rationalize seeing his dad for the first time in three years. That part of the past still stung, even though he had therapy and went to the A.A. meetings. The abuse was something that would always be a part of him. He decided to stop by the local ABC store to grab a bottle of vodka, using a fake ID. He then decided to drive back home in hopes that he would bypass his dad. He hid the vodka bottle in his jacket and went directly to his room. He decided not to drink that night, so he just hid the bottle under his bed. He wrote and drew how he felt since being back in PA. The drawing and writing reflected all the bottled-up, unresolved emotions from the last three years. Healing would be a process, and he could feel himself slipping back into his old patterns.

* * *

Chase hadn't seen his friends, Bryce, Hunter, Landon, and Tristan for three years. He decided to give them a call to see if they wanted to catch up. His friends were very eager to see him after all these years, so of course, when he called them, they all agreed to meet up.

So that afternoon, Chase and his friends ended up at the local diner, eating and catching up on old times. They were all in college now, Bryce was studying to be an engineer. Hunter was studying to be a medical technician. Landon was studying to be lawyer. Tristan was studying to be a chemist. They each talked about how college was for them and that Chase didn't know what he was missing.

"So where were you these few years, you disappeared on us?" Bryce asked

"I went to live with my aunt in CA, family issues," he stated, not fully wanting to get into much detail. "How are you guys doing, other than school? Any girlfriends?"

"Hunter has a girl. Her name is Bailey," Landon said.

"We've been together for a year and a half, and it's pretty serious," Hunter said.

"How about you? Did you meet anyone while in CA?" Tristan jumped in.

"No, no, I didn't, meet anyone while I was out there. I focused on other things. I didn't have time for a girlfriend."

"Since you are back, we'll keep an eye out for you," Bryce said with a smirk.

"Geez, thanks," Chase said sarcastically.

The boys finished eating, and each paid for their meal. After they paid, they stayed in the diner and continued to talk and catch up. Then Tristan said, "Hey, guys, want to go to the movies to see 'The End Game?" he asked.

"Isn't that the long movie?" Hunter said uninterested. "I'd rather have sex with my girlfriend."

"I'm interested," said Tristan

"So am I," said Chase.

"It's settled, let's go," said Bryce. "Hunter, you can go have sex with your girlfriend, while we go watch the movie," Bryce joked. The others laughed.

"All right, all right...I'll go. But I better not fall asleep." Hunter said, giving in to their demand.

So, Chase and his friends left the diner and headed to the store to buy a whole bunch of snacks to take inside the movie. They drove to the theater, got their tickets, and went in. Three hours later, they all came out the theater raving about the movie.

"Wasn't that movie better than sex with your girlfriend, Hunter?" Bryce said, not letting him live down his comment from earlier.

"No comment," Hunter said, while Chase and Landon both laughed hysterically.

"Hey guys," Tristan interrupted their laughing, "Do you want to come over my house? We can have time to relax and chill?"

All of them knew what he was referring to when he said relax and chill. They all echoed, "Sure." After they left the theater, they each got into their cars and drove to Tristan's house. His parents were gone on a business trip, so they had the house all to themselves. Tristan told them that they could sit on the couch and turn the music channel on, that he would be back. So, Chase, Bryce, Landon and Hunter, all sat talking about the movie and listening to emo/rock music. It seemed like it was taking forever for Tristan to come back from his room. When he finally did, he had barbiturates, codeine, Percocet, Vicodin, and some other unknown types of drugs in his hand.

"Dude, what the hell, what is all of this?" Bryce said, looking at all the drugs he had.

"Don't worry about it. Do you want some?" he asked each one of his friends.

"Hell yeah," they all said in unison.

So, they all sat around getting drunk and high and eating the leftover snacks they bought for the movie. After a while of this, they all passed out, some on the couch, some on the floor.

The next morning, they sobered up and cleaned the living room to where there was no evidence of their partying last night. Last night was a blur to all of them. They all stayed for an hour before leaving Tristan's house.

Chase was the first one to leave Tristan's house. Before he left, he told them he has a great time hanging and that they have to get together more often. They all agreed to set up a time for the next hang out.

He got into his father's mustang and drove home. He parked beside his dad's truck. He then got out and proceeded to walk up to his front door and unlock it. Upon entering, his mother was sitting watching tv. She heard the door open.

"Chase, where were you? I called your cell like a thousand times, each time it went to voicemail," she said angrily.

"Mom, I stayed over Tristan's house last night, my phone was off," Chase said apologetically.

"I was worried sick about you," she added.

"Mom, I'm fine, don't you think I'm old enough to take care of myself," he reasoned.

"Yes, honey, but next time tell me where you are going," she explained.

"All right," he said just to appease her.

"You haven't seen your dad since you got back to PA. He's upstairs getting ready to go to the gallery. Maybe you to could hang out together at the gallery and catch up. He missed you a lot too, Chase."

"I'll pass," Chase said rather coldly.

"Chase, whatever you have against your father, you have to resolve it," she added.

"You're really in denial, mom. It's a shame," he stated and left her to go to his room.

Dana just shook her head and continued to watch her daytime shows. Ethan then came downstairs and saw his wife watching tv.

"Was that the door?" he asked.

"Yes, it was Chase. He's up in his room, right now," she answered.

"Oh, well is he coming with me to the gallery?" he asked

her. "You told him, I wanted to catch up with him and have a father and son day, right?"

"He doesn't want to go right now. He just spent the night at Tristan's house. I think he is too tired for that," she said sort of lying.

"Oh, all right. Well, I'll be back around 5pm. I'll bring dinner home," he said as he kissed her softly.

Chase was in his room drawing and writing in his journal. He was still a little high off the drugs he took at Tristan's house. It showed in the dark colors, reds, blues, and blacks he chose to draw with. He remembered the poster on Dr. C's wall that said, 'The wound may have not been your fault, but healing is your responsibility.' He quickly jogged that down in his notebook and circled in bold marker 'healing is your responsibility.' He understood that, but he didn't know how he would take hold of his healing when he hated his father so much.

He was drawing and writing when he heard footsteps coming up the stairs towards his room. The door opened. It was his father. Chase froze. He hasn't been in the same room as his father in three years. Chase immediately closed his journal. He was afraid to look at his father, in fear that all his bottled-up anger would surface, and he would just go off on him. So, Chase just got up and left his room, leaving his dad there.

His dad stood silently for a minute, looking around Chase's room. He then turned around, went downstairs, and grabbed his keys. He had told Dana he would bring dinner home, that he was going out with his artist friends, and not to wait up for him.

* * *

Chase sat on the couch engrossed in his music. It was an escape for him, like drawing and writing was. He felt helpless, helpless talking to his mother, helpless not wanting to face his father. His friends didn't even know what happened to him as a teenager. Maybe it was time to come clean to them, maybe they could offer some solace for him. He decided to text Bryce, told him to meet him at the local tattoo parlor 'Skull and Bones Ink.'

Chase waited in his car for fifteen minutes outside of the tattoo parlor when Bryce finally pulled up. Bryce stepped out of his car and hopped into Chase's car.

"What's up, Bro? Deciding to get a tattoo? And needed moral support?" he asked.

"Sort of... I brought you out here to tell you something I've been harboring since I was a teenager," Chase explained.

"Chase, dude, you know you can tell me anything, we're like brothers," he reassured him.

"I know that, Bryce, this is very difficult for me to say, because it doesn't happen to guys very often," he said.

"Whatever it is, you can tell me," Bryce explained.

"I was physically abused by my father," Chase admitted to him.

"What, what the hell, Chase why are you just telling me now? Do you want me to kick his ass? Because I will," he said sternly.

"No, no, I appreciate that gesture, but I just wanted to tell someone who would listen without judgment," he explained.

"Of course, no problem, man, if you ever want to talk about it with me, I will gladly listen. Now, since we are here, are you planning to get a tattoo?" He added.

"Yes, I am, and you are my moral support," he said, laughing.

They both entered the tattoo shop and went to the counter where this heavily pierced and tattooed guy asked who was getting a tattoo? Chase replied, "I am. He's my friend, and he came for moral support."

"Do you need to look through designs?" the guy asked Chase.

"No, I want the words "Your wound is probably not your fault, but your healing is your responsibility."

"Ok, no problem, where do you want it placed on your body?" he asked.

"My forearm," Chase responded.

Bryce waited out in the lobby area until Chase was done.

"Did it hurt?" he asked.

"Not really," Chase answered." Want to see?"

"Sure," said Bryce

Chase rolled back his sleeve and showed the saying in beautifully scripted letters.

"That's so awesome, I love it Chase," Bryce exclaimed.

Chase then paid for the tattoo and thanked the artist who did it. He and Bryce left and stood in front of the shop, they exchanged a brotherly hug, each got in their cars and drove to their respective destinations.

Chase got home when his mom had already gone to bed. So, he ate the shrimp and seafood platter his dad brought home for dinner. After he ate, took a shower, washed his hair, and was careful not to get his new tattoo wet. He put his pj's on and climbed into his bed. He took one last look at his fresh new ink and said to himself, healing is my responsibility. I will heal from this. The tattoo was his constant reminder.

8

TORMENTED THOUGHTS: A TICKING TIME BOMB

Chase woke to nineteen balloons placed strategically all around his room and a card on his dresser. He sat up in his bed and looked around at his birthday balloons. *Mom did this* he thought to himself. He got up to get the card off his dresser to read, when his mom came in with the breakfast she made for him.

"Happy birthday," she smiled and gave him a hug and a kiss. "Here I made breakfast for you," she added.

"Thanks, mom, I love you," he replied.

"Rest up, honey. Later your father and I are going to take you out to eat."

"Umm... okay," he said. Not really wanting to celebrate with his father, but he looked down at his tattoo and remembered.

He checked his texts and voicemails. He had a lot of texts from family members and friends. His aunt Sarah left him the sweetest birthday message on his voicemail. *Today is shaping up to be a great day*, he thought.

He finished the breakfast his mom made him, took a shower, and got dressed. He got a text from Bryce as soon as he stepped out of the shower. He wanted to see if Chase wanted to go to the mall and shop. Chase replied "Yes, are Tristan, Landon, and Hunter coming?"

Bryce texted back, "Duh, of course, it's your birthday! Meet us at the mall around 1:30 pm."

Chase went downstairs and saw his mother sitting at the kitchen table looking through a photo book of Chase when he was a baby. He stepped slowly behind her shoulder, peeking down at the book. She felt him looking over her shoulder.

"Chase, you were a cute baby!" she gushed.

"What, I'm not cute now?" he joked.

"You know what I mean, and yes, you are so adorable now," she said.

"Mom, my friends and I are going to go to the mall around 1:30 pm. What time do you plan on taking me out for my birthday?" he asked.

"Around 3:00pm, your father gets home from the gallery early today."

"Oh all right, we'll only be a couple of hours."

"Have fun and be safe," she cautioned.

"I will."

He left the house and drove to the mall. Bryce told him to meet them in front of the entrance. When he saw them, they all shouted 'Happy Birthday' in unison.

"Thank you, thanks guys," he replied.

"We should all go to a strip club tonight," Hunter suggested

"And your girlfriend would love that," Landon said sarcastically

"Umm...it's not for me. It's for Chase," he snarked back.

"Yeah, oooook," Bryce chimed in.

"As much as I want to take you guys up on this offer, my parents are taking me out this afternoon, and I want to spend some time with them," he stated. "Maybe some other time."

"Let's go, we are wasting time standing around," Hunter replied.

Chase and his friends entered the mall. First, they went to the sneaker store and browsed the latest sneakers. Then they went to a few clothing stores, where Chase brought a new outfit. Finally, they stopped by the gaming store, to browse through the latest Xbox games. They shopped and joked around a lot. Two hours just flew by, and soon it was time to leave. They all wished Chase a 'Happy Birthday' again and to enjoy his birthday outing with his parents.

"Raincheck, on the strip club," Hunter yelled out to Chase as he was walking to his car.

Chase yelled back, "Of course..."

Chase had to get home and get ready to go out with his parents for his birthday. His mother and father were ready and waiting downstairs for him to come from the mall.

"You ready?" they said in unison.

"Let me quickly freshen up," Chase responded as he rushed upstairs to change.

Fifteen minutes later, Chase came down wearing a new outfit and sneakers he brought from the mall.

"You look amazing." His mother said.

"Agreed, cool outfit," his father echoed.

"You guys ready? Where are we going to eat?" Chase asked.

"Hibachi grill, since I know how you love Asian food," his mom answered.

"Let's go. I'm ready to eat," Chase said.

On the way to the hibachi grill, there was a strange eerie silence. Chase really didn't want his father to be here, but his mother wouldn't have had it any other way. The tension grew as they got closer to the place. They pulled up to the restaurant and got out. Chase's mother whispered something to his father, and he disappeared into the restaurant.

Soon Chase and his mother entered the restaurant. The waiter, who got the number of people from his father, told them to follow him. When they got to the table, it was decorated with balloons and a sign that said, 'Happy Birthday Chase.'

"You like it?" his mother asked.

"Yes, thanks, mom."

The waiter motioned them to sit, he had three menus placed in front of them. He then proceeded to tell them about the specials on the menu and asked them for their drink order.

"Water," Chase's mom told the waiter.

"I'll have a beer," Chase's father told the waiter

"I'll have a coke," Chase told the waiter

"Ok, I'll give you a few minutes to look at the menu, then I'll be back in a few," said the waiter as he proceeded to leave.

Everyone was engrossed in the menu and trying to find what they wanted to eat. After ten minutes, everyone knew what that were getting to eat, the waiter finally came back with their drinks, and asked if they were ready to order. They were, so the waiter went around the table and took their orders and left to put them in.

"So how was your day today, Chase?" his father broke the tension.

"It was ok, no big deal," he answered reluctantly.

"You are almost out of your teens," he told him.

"And that's a big deal," his mom interjected.

"Not to me. It's like any other day," he said.

Soon the food arrived, and everyone was concerned with eating, that the conversation was little to none. Chase just wanted to go home. It made his stomach turn to be in the same room as his father. Chase downed the coke and took his mind off of the present moment.

"Can I be excused? I need to use the bathroom," Chase asked his parents.

"Sure, honey, hurry back. I think there is some cake coming out for you," his mom hinted.

Chase rushed to the bathroom, inside the stall, he text Tristan to ask him about some pills, and he told him to meet him in the bathroom of the hibachi grill. In fifteen minutes, Tristan entered the bathroom where Chase was, handed him some pills, then snuck back out.

Chase left the bathroom and went back to the table where his parents were. There was a huge cake waiting for him.

"What took you so long, Chase?" his mother asked.

"Umm... when you have to go, you have to go," he replied.

"Say no more," his dad interjected.

"Happy birthday, Chase," the waiter exclaimed.

"Thanks, everyone. I appreciate all the love."

"Make a wish!" the waiter said excitedly.

Chase decided not to make a wish and just blew out the candles. "Can't we just take the cake home? I had a long day, and I'm tired," Chase pleaded.

"Sure, honey," his mother motioned to the waiter the box up the cake.

As soon as the waiter left to put the cake in a box, Chase's father went up to the front to pay for the food. The waiter came back with the boxed cake and handed it over to Dana. He wished another Happy Birthday to Chase and left to attend to other waiting customers.

The drive home was again plagued with eerie silence. As soon as they arrived home, Chase went straight to his room. He couldn't take being around his father. He felt like he was going to have a panic attack. The suppressed tormenting thoughts he heard earlier during dinner, got louder, and louder. He wanted to put an end to these thoughts, once and for all. He took the pills Tristan gave him at the Hibachi grill and downed it with the vodka he has stashed under his bed. He took scissors that he has on his desk and started to cut himself. He made little drawings on his skin, blood dripping on to the carpet. He then passed out on the floor.

Dana was downstairs looking through Chase's school-age photos with her husband. Reminiscing about how Chase was as a kindergartener through a 5th grade student. Dana wanted to show Chase his school-age photos, so she yelled for him to come downstairs. She yelled three times, and he didn't come, so she went upstairs to his room and opened the door. When she opened the door, she let out a scream, and she yelled "Ethan call 911."

The ambulance soon arrived and took Chase to the hospital. At the hospital, Chase had a psychiatric evaluation, one thing that the hospital in CA, didn't perform. The doctors told Chase's parents the reason why they are giving Chase a psychiatric evaluation is because he had prior scars on his arms and drugs in his system.

Chase's parents were questioned by the doctors and had to fill out paperwork for him to go to a local psychiatric ward. They ordered him to be admitted right away because of the severity of his situation.

They explained that this wasn't his first suicide attempt and that he most likely tried to commit suicide, two times before this attempt.

"He just came from living with my sister in CA. She had spoken to me about how she couldn't deal with his behavior and mentioned the two previous suicide attempts," Dana explained.

"Why wasn't he living with you, his parents, why his aunt?" the doctors questioned.

"Well, umm...he was very rebellious. He refused to listen to us, so we sent him to live with my wife's sister," Chase's dad said, lying to the doctor.

"Well, whatever the case was, I'm ordering him to be admitted immediately to a psychiatric ward to get the help he needs," the doctor explained.

"Thank you, doctor, we appreciate you wanting to help

our son. We hate that he had to go through this," Chase's mom said gratefully.

"No problem, it's our job," the doctor reassured her.

"Can we go in to see him now?" they asked.

"Yes, you may go in and see him," the doctor said.

"You go, darling, I will wait out here in the lobby," Ethan told her.

"All right," she said, kissing his forehead.

Dana quietly entered Chase's hospital room, where he was just resting peacefully. He looked like an angel, his mom thought to herself. She couldn't believe her baby wanted to take his own life for the third time. She thought carefully about the words she would say. She didn't want to say anything to trigger him because of his fragile state right now. She decided to wait until he had spoken first. She just sat and look at him.

"Mom," he finally spoke, "I'm sorry. I'll..." his voice trailed off.

'Shh...honey, it's okay. You don't have to explain," she said, going over to him. She rubbed his hair and kissed his forehead. "I love you, Chase. You just made a desperate choice that could have taken you from us. We are going to get you the help you need," she explained.

"The doctor said you need to be admitted to a psychiatric ward. Chase, I can't help you, as bad as I want to. I hate seeing you in pain, but your father and I can't give you the true help you need," she told him.

Chase was just listening to his mother talk. He knew he needed help and admitted to himself that he cannot deal with his past abuse solely on his own. Maybe going to a psych ward would be the best option right now.

"Yes, I will go. I want to get help," he told his mom.

"I love you so much, I just want you to get better," she explained

"I do too," he said.

When his mother left the room, he looked down at his tattoo that was now covered in fresh scars from his self-harming and was determined to fully heal. No matter how long it took.

The doctor told him and his parents that the psychiatric ward was expecting him this evening and that he had to be admitted immediately. He didn't even tell his friends about his ordeal, he just wanted to keep it to himself for the time being

Dana was upset that she would be separated from her son once more. She didn't know for how long, and even though it was painful. She knew he needed this help. Chase knew it too.

"I love you, mom. It will be okay. I will get the help I need and be a better son to you," he said.

"Oh, Chase, you are already the best son a mother could ask for. We will get through this together. We will be stronger as a family because of it," she added.

The doctor's told Chase's mom that she needed to get clothes for him to wear during his hospital stay and that he not allowed to have his cell phone on him. The hospital is very strict about enforcing the rules to keep everyone safe, and to not worry too much about him, that he will be getting the best care he needs for his healing.

9

ARTISTIC SOULS: THE MEETING OF THE MINDS

"Rain, I need you to sign some papers. You will be admitted for a week's stay. And then we will take it from there regarding discharging you when the week in through," the case manger explained.

"Okay," she said.

The case manager sorted through each of the papers and showed Rain where she needed to sign. Rain signed all the paperwork and was explained the policies and procedures of the facility. She was also given a packet to review what she'd been told.

"Nurse Jones will show you around the facility and to your room," a lady who appeared to be in her late 40s with brown hair and olive skin came into the little office. She was carrying a note pad that had the patient's name and room numbers on it. The nurse came up behind Rain and touched her shoulder to motion her to come,"

"Hi Rain," she said. "I'm Nurse Jones. I will be showing you around the facility and to your room."

They both exited the office and walked down the small hallway. The walls were white like a hospital would be. The was a huge whiteboard with the daily happenings of the facility. Each room they passed had been uniquely set up by the patients who occupied the rooms. Rain carefully looked inside the rooms but not a lingering look for fear the other patients would get upset. She wanted to know when she was coming up to her room. As soon as the thought crossed her mind, Nurse Jones said, "Here we are."

Rain entered into the one bedroom. She requested to have no roommate. She wanted her privacy and was glad she opted for that choice. As she entered, she noticed the walls were painted a cream color and had pictures of flowers framed hanging around the room. There was a white desk against the front wall with plain white paper stacked on top. She noticed the bed with a white hospital looking sheets on it and a thick, heavy throw cover on the end of the bed in case it got chilly. She glanced at the two windows. They had blinds the same color as the room's wall. On the side where the desk was, there was an open closet for her clothes and what other things she brought with her. Surveying the room, she didn't think it would be so bad here. She volunteered to come here to be healed, and that's what she was going to do.

"Ready? I will show you where you dine," Nurse Jones said.

"I'm ready."

After leaving her room, they continued to walk until they got to this big room where about twenty people were hanging out playing board games and reading books or magazines. The other patients' eyes were on her.

"And this is our multipurpose room. It's where you eat, have snacks, and all the classes are at, like arts and crafts."

"Hey, Nurse Jones, who's the new girl," yelled one of the patients as the others were looking on.

"This is Rain. She just came in today. I want you guys to be especially nice to her," said Nurse Jones.

"Hi Rain," they all say in unison.

"Hi," Rain said back

They all went back to doing what they are doing.

Nurse Jones explained, "It's free recreation time where the patients play board games, read, and talk among themselves. We don't clean up and have dinner until 5:30 pm."

"What do you want to do? Stay here or go back to your room? I can walk you back, if you want," Nurse Jones said politely.

"I'll stay here," Rain insisted.

"Ok, I'll be at the nurse's station if you need me. Then, Nurse Jones exited out the door, leaving Rain to survey the entire room full of people.

They looked normal, she thought. She surveyed the entire room when her eye caught a boy sitting by himself who was looked to be writing or drawing something. He looked about her age, he had a long sleeved black sabbath shirt on and baggy semi ripped jeans. He had long, shaggy cut, black hair, and piercing blue eyes. She walked over to him, and he looked up from what he was doing.

"Hi, my name is Rain. How are you?" she said politely

"I know, I heard the nurse say your name when she introduced you, I'm fine. The name is Chase." he said rather matter of factly.

"Nice to meet you, Chase. May I sit down with you?" she said

"Sure, I guess," he replied. She sat down next to him and noticed his drawing. "That's neat," she commented.

"Thanks, it's a knife that's piercing through a bloodied heart," he said

"Oh," she didn't know what else to say.

Then she proceeded to ask, "What landed you in here?"

He didn't look at her for a second because he was into his drawing. He then stopped drawing and lifted up his one shirt sleeve. It was covered in scars some fresh, some healed over. Rain was taken back. She just looked at his arm and didn't say another word.

Over the loud speaker, one of the nurses announced dinner would be in an hour. After the announcement, everyone started to clean up and disperse back to their rooms.

Suddenly, Rain found herself in an empty room. She slowly got up, looked around at the half cleaned up room, and proceeded to walk back to her room alone. She got back to her room and looked through her bags to find her grandmother's bible. She missed her grandparents so much. They would have not wanted to see her like this. Not only was she dealing with their deaths, she was dealing with the fact she had been raped and the inner healing and forgiveness that had to take place regarding that. She knew the only comfort she had was God's word. She found the scripture that was her comfort during this time, that God was close to the broken hearted and saves those who are crushed in spirit. She meditated on that and let the words soothe her. She then proceeded to close her grandmother's bible and put it on the desk. I should unpack she thought. She proceeded to pull her clothes from her bag, fold them, and put them away.

As she was putting the last article of clothing in her drawer, she heard the nurse on the loud speaker. All patients proceeded to the dining area for dinner. She put the articles of clothing away and went to the dining room.

The patients were filing in slowing, as they had to wait in line to get their food from the staff on duty. "Maggie, Emma, John, Stacy, Chase, Rain," the staff called the patients one by one.

Rain got her tray and took a seat at the nearest table. Soon after she sat down, Maggie and Emma joined her at the table. They smiled and introduced themselves to Rain. Maggie was bipolar, and Emma had anorexia, and she had to be monitored closely to make sure she ate all her food. Rain was relieved. She thought she'd never make friends after that incident with Chase earlier. Speaking of Chase, he sat with two of his pals, laughing and joking, Rain wondered what was really going on in his head, those scars he showed her earlier bothered her. She decided that she would pray for him, and that if he wanted to open up to her, he would.

Rain had the best pizza in the world. It was a cheese pizza with a side of garlic bread. She was surprised that the hospital food tasted so awesome. She was told by the nurse earlier that she could order her food from now on, that since she just came in this afternoon, it was too late to order. Maggie and Emma had finished their food and were talking amongst themselves, waiting for Rain to finish. Rain proceeded to take the last bite of her garlic bread and clean up her tray to hand back to the staff. Maggie, Emma, and Rain all picked up their trays and stood in line to turn them in.

"Excellent, Emma," a male staff member said.

Emma smiled and handed him her tray, followed by Maggie, then Rain.

"Was it good?" he said to Rain.

"Why yes, yes it was," she replied.

After the girls handed in their trays, Rain proceeded to ask what happens next to Maggie.

"Well, we usually go back to our rooms or hang out here until visiting hours, which is 7-9pm."

"Oh ok, I don't think I'll have any visitors today, but I could be wrong," she said.

"We're going to stay here," said Emma.

"We usually play a board game and wait for our families to arrive," Maggie said. "Stay with us and play a game."

"Well, okay," Rain said to them. They proceeded to pull out 'scrabble' and start to play that.

Not too long into the game, they saw the patients' families start to come in. One by one, they joined their families and started talking to them. All you could hear was low whispering voices.

When Emma and Maggie went to their respective families, Rain just grabbed a magazine and started reading it. Soon she saw a man, about in his late thirties dressed in jeans and a sweatshirt standing in the doorway. The nurse whispered something to him, and he nodded his head. The man called out to Chase. Everyone looked up at the man. Chase was too busy writing and drawing to notice. The man called out again. Chase got up and stormed out of the room, pushing the man, almost off his feet. The nurse had to catch him. Chase stormed to his room and slammed his door shut. Everyone soon turned back to talking with their families, like nothing happened. The nurse whispered something else to the man, and then they left.

Who was that man and why did Chase storm out of the room like that? Rain wondered.

Praying for him was definitely a great idea. She went back to reading the magazine, but she was very concerned about what just took place. She couldn't shake it. She felt bothered by it. She wanted to talk with Chase to see why he did that. She made up in her mind that she would start praying for Chase and all of the patients here. Visiting hours were almost over, and the patients' families were filing out the facility. Emma kissed her family members, and Maggie did the same. Then their family members left. They walked over to Rain to say that they were heading to their rooms. They cleaned up the game of scrabble, and then Maggie and Emma headed to their rooms. Rain decided to stay and watch Tv. Some of the other patients joined her, but she was still worried about Chase.

Meanwhile, Chase came walking by and went into the other common area of the hospital. Rain slowly got up and followed him into the other common area. This area was a lot smaller. It had a TV, books, and movies stacked on a shelf. It also had a little couch that you could sit on. When she got there, she waited a second to go in. She slowly opened the door and sat on the couch directly next to Chase. He seemed to be engrossed in a book. So, she just sat there watching tv, which was on the Nick channel. Spongebob was on. She couldn't wait any longer to break the ice with Chase, so she just came out and said it.

"Was that your father that came to visit you tonight?"

"Yes," he replied. "We aren't on speaking terms. We haven't been for a while," he added.

"Oh, do you mind if I ask why not?" she asked.

He hesitated at first, then spoke. "He beat me when I was growing up. I've never got over that. I had three suicide attempts. The third attempt landed me here. Every time I see him, the memories flood back, and I lose it. I hate him so much," he said. "It's hard for me to forgive him or my mom for not believing me and staying with him."

"Oh Chase, I know it's hard, but you must. The bible says you have to forgive in order for God to forgive you. I'm learning this very aspect too. I know it's easier said than done," she said empathically.

"Yeah, I'm not religious like you, so I don't believe that. I believe in getting even," he said.

Rain didn't know what else to say, but she knew if Chase was ever going to forgive anyone, he'd have to learn the forgiving power of God first, and that could take a while.

"So why are you here?" he asked Rain.

"Well on top on dealing with the death of my grandparents, I was raped by a college classmate not too long ago. I went to a sexual assault survivors' group and heard them talking about this facility and decided to check myself in here."

"Oh my God. I'm so sorry. How can some guy be so sick

to do that to a woman," Chase said. "Are you close to your parents?" he asked.

"Very. I'm very close to my parents. I love them so much, and I thank God for them every day," she said.

"That's awesome," he said.

Then, the nurse on the loud speaker came on. "Lights out in five minutes."

"I guess we'd better get going back to our rooms," he said.

"I guess we better."

They both got up and said their goodbyes and went to their respective rooms.

In her room, Rain was thinking on the conversation that she and Chase had. She got her PJ's on and crawled into her bed. She silently prayed for Chase, then she fell fast asleep.

10

THE PRAYER THAT CHANGED A HEART

The next morning, Rain woke up around 6 am, read her grandmother's bible, and prayed. After that, she got her clothes out for the day and hopped in the shower. Five minutes later after she got out of the shower, one of the staff came on the speaker and said breakfast was ready in the dining area. She rushed to put on her clothes and head down to breakfast. She was ready to eat. She was starving, and she knew she ordered pancakes, bacon, and hash browns. Just thinking about it made her hungry.

Down at the dining room, some of the patients were fully dressed, some had their pj's still on. But everyone seemed to be in a great mood this morning. She spotted Emma and Maggie who saved her a seat their table. She went to get her tray and sat down with them.

"Hi guys," Rain said cheerfully. "How are you this morning?"

"Fine," Maggie said.

"I'm fine," Emma also said.

Rain looked around for Chase but didn't see him at any of the tables. She wondered if he was all right. She went back to eating her breakfast. When she finished, she handed in her tray, told the girls that she would see them later, and went back to her room. In her room, she decided to draw. She had not drawn in a while. She went out to ask the staff at the desk for some pencils. She got them and she went back to her room, sat down at the desk, and began to draw. She drew God's hands holding up a boy with long shaggy cut black hair, with scars on his arms, and a big hole in his heart. She felt that Chase needed to see this drawing, but only when the time was right.

"Rain," she heard over the loud speaker, "medication time." She got up from drawing and went to the nurse's station. One of the nurses handed her a small white pill. She took it, and then drunk the water that was given to her afterward.

"Stretching will be in fifteen minutes. Many of the patients enjoy stretching. It helps their anxiety and clears their mind," one of the nurses told her.

"Oh okay... I think I will try it," Rain said to the nurse. She then proceeded down to the multipurpose room. When she got there, all the chairs were in a circle and that patients were signing into the class. Rain went over to sign her name and room number. After she looked around, she saw Chase and an empty chair next to him, so she came and sat down. He looked a little better emotion wise than from the conversation they had the day before. But again, maybe that was an act. She couldn't tell. Chase gave her a half-smile and the class begun.

After class, everyone was talking about how great it was. Rain even went up to the instructor and thanked her for a great class. After she finished talking with the instructor, she went over to Chase to see what he thought about it. He wasn't really responding to her questions and barely looking her in the eyes. She then grabbed his arm to signal she was there for him if he needed her. He cringed and snatched his arm back. She looked at the hurt in his eyes, but she didn't say anything and let him go. He finished putting his chair back and left, leaving her standing all alone.

She then just walked out and went to her room. She continued to work on the drawing, reading her bible, and praying. She was told visiting hours were earlier today, from 2-4pm. She went to call her mom to see if she was going to come visit, and she said yes, that she was missing her and would bring her whatever she needed. Rain was very excited to see her mother. She knew talking with her would ease her mind about everything.

She finished up her drawing and reading when a knock on the door was heard. She opened it, and there stood her mother with concern in her eyes for her daughter.

They embraced for what seemed like an eternity. After the embrace, they sat in Rain's room to catch up.

"How is everything going?" Rain's mom asked her.

"It's going. How did you get to come visit? It's after visiting hours," she asked.

"Nurse Jones, made an exception for me only for tonight. How are doing? How are the other patients towards you?"

"I'm doing fine. It's a process. I have my good days and bad days. The staff here are very helpful and supportive.

Healing is on your own terms. There is no one size fits all when it comes to healing from a traumatic experience. I just have to take it one day at a time. The other patients are cool, we each share an unspoken bond that connect us in that we are all healing from something," she added.

"Your father and I miss you so much. We're taking this in our stride as well. We just want you to get better. Here is the things, you told me to bring to you," Her mom said as she handed her a bag.

"Thank you, mom. I appreciate it.

"Well, I have to go. It's getting late. I love you".

"I love you too," Rain said as she hugged her once again before she left.

She felt good about her visit with her mother. After the visit, she decided to take a nap for a little while until dinner. She couldn't wait until dinner. She ordered them lemon peppered fish with corn and broccoli. *Yum...* she thought. She then proceeded to drift off to sleep. She woke up at 4:45 pm. She freshened up and read for a little while until 5:30 pm and headed to dinner. At dinner she met with Maggie and Emma again, talked, ate, and was acting silly with them. But in the back of her mind, she wondered what Chase was thinking and what was going on in his mind. She saw him over there with his friends laughing and joking, she caught his eye, but he looked down to the floor. He looked back up again and continued to talk among his friends.

After dinner, she decided to go to the small common area

hoping Chase would stop in. When he didn't, she went back to the larger common area and sat and prayed. She looked outside the window at the lights that lit up the night sky. After a while, she looked up, and there in the doorway was Chase. She could tell he was having a rough time. She had to show him the picture she drew, but it was in her room. So she told Chase that she wanted to show him something, to wait here, she had to back to her room to get it. She came back to sit beside Chase with the drawing.

He asked, "So what is it you want to show me?"

"This," she said and handed him the picture she drew of him and God's hands.

He looked at it for a long moment and smiled, then he broke down crying. "This is amazing" he spoke through his tears.

He looked at the drawing more intently. He could see she put a lot of effort into this drawing, like it was especially drawn for him. "Thank you, this is really very special to me. No one has ever drawn something so meaningful."

"You're very welcome Chase. I wanted to show you that you're not alone in your fight for healing. I'm here for you, and God is here for you too." She explained.

"I appreciate that Rain, I know in the beginning I was a little standoffish, and I apologize for that. You've proven to be a great friend to me, and I just want to say thank you."

She was overjoyed, but she kept her emotions at bay. Rain was on cloud nine. She couldn't believe God was answering her prayers, and she could feel herself falling for Chase.

At breakfast, she sat with Chase and his friends. She

could see God working on Chase's heart. After breakfast, she and Chase went to the little room, watched TV, and talked. No one bothered them, not the staff or the nurses. Some of the patients could see a friendship developing between Chase and Rain. Some of them were not happy about this. They knew where Chase came from, but they didn't know what was happening in Chase's heart, and what God was healing him from, his dark past. Rain knew that so she didn't mind dealing with the naysayers.

During breakfast, Chase told Rain that said he was ready to face his father and mother and forgive them both for what they'd done. Rain told him that she would pray for that meeting. She told him that God would show up and work in the midst of the conversation with his father and mother.

Then, 7 o'clock rolled around. Chase and Rain were sitting reading Rain's grandmother's bible. Rain reassured Chase that whatever happened between the conversation with his mother and father, God would be with him. Rain saw her mother and father out the corner of her eye, and she motioned them to come over. She introduced them to Chase and squeezed Chase's hand before leaving him to go meet with her parents.

As soon as she left, Chase's dad showed up with the nurse again. They whispered to one another.

Chase proceeded to walk slowly to his dad.

"Can we go somewhere to talk," he asked his dad.

"Sure, son. I've been wanting to get things off my chest, that I've been holding on to."

They both walked to the large common area to continue to talk.

"Let me go first, Chase, I'm sorry. I'm sorry I hurt you and caused you pain all these years. I didn't know any better. I was selfish, and I'm sorry. Will you forgive me?" he added

"Yes, I forgive you," Chase said as he hugged his father

His father embraced him back, and they both started to cry.

This was the first step in the healing process for Chase. Soon after his mother joined in the conversation and Chase embraced and forgave her as well.

11

THE JOURNEY TO HEALING

After Chase finished talking with his parents, he came back into the dining room where Rain and her family were sitting, and he told her thank you. He thanked her for teaching him how to forgive and the importance of forgiveness regarding the healing process. The nurse called Chase and his family to a meeting to see when he would get discharged and the next logical steps from there.

They soon disappeared from sight. Rain continued to talk with her mother and father. She couldn't tell them what the next step in the healing process was for her. She felt she still needed to work through some unresolved issues.

"I think I need more time in here," she said honestly to her parents.

"You do? I understand if you aren't really to leave yet, your healing in our top priority too," her mom said.

A staff member motioned to her and her family to have a meeting to see if she can get discharged soon as well.

They both had their family meetings. Chase got the go

ahead to be discharged. But Rain and her family decided that she needed more time. Chase's family went to his room to gather his things, at least everything except what he needed for the next day. After their families left, Rain and Chase were alone again. They walked hand in hand to the little common area to sit down and talk.

"Rain," Chase began. "I will never forget this experience. You taught me so much about myself and the areas I needed to work on in my life.

"You're welcome, but it wasn't me. It was God who opened your heart to forgive. I'm going to miss you, Chase. I wish this wasn't goodbye."

"It doesn't have to be, Rain. I will still try and visit you here. Like you, I have a lot of work ahead of me, the counseling with my family and continuing to heal."

"I know," she said. "I want to be there for you every step of the way."

"And I want to be there for you as well," Chase echoed.

He saw a pad and a pen on the desk, wrote down his contact information, and gave it to her. Afterward, she took a piece of paper, wrote down hers, and gave it to him. They hugged, then they went to their separate rooms.

* * *

The next morning, she heard a knock at the door. She went and got the door. And there stood Chase dressed in an orange t-shirt with a long-sleeved gray zip-up hoodie and baggy jeans. His hair was kind of messy, but Rain loved it that way.

"Hey," he said as he embraced her.

"Hey yourself," she giggled. "Are you all packed and ready to go?"

"Yes," he said. "I'm just thinking about what I have to do once I leave. It's still going to be a challenge for me, my road of healing is just beginning,"

"I know, it's going to be tough, but you guys will get through it," she reassured him.

"I will miss you, Rain. But I know you have to heal as well, and I will try and visit you when I can, but also give you space to completely heal."

"Let's have our last breakfast together," he said as they walked hand and hand to the dining area.

Chase and Rain found a little corner of the dining area and sat down to eat. Chase's friends came up with things they made in the art classes for him to take home.

As soon as breakfast was over, Chase and Rain went to the small multipurpose room to be alone. They sat and talked about the experiences they had while here. They were thankful to have met each other and excited about their budding friendship.

"I will call you tomorrow," he said.

"I'll look forward to that," she answered.

Keep reading for a special preview of the sequel in the "Artistic Series"
By
Regina Ann Faith
Coming in 2020

They'd come a long way since the days at the hospital. Both Rain and Chase began dating shortly after. Rain, finished up community college, earned her A.A in Art and now worked part-time in Chase's father's art gallery 'Stroke of the Brush'. Chase also displayed his art at his father's art gallery, when they did art shows. Rain and Chase also volunteer in their local church, sharing their testimony with the youth and young adults. Chase's relationship with his parents have mended, thanks to counseling which they still attended off and on. Rain still went to the sexual assault survivors group, and eventually shared her story with the women, who became like her second family. Their lives seem to be like a fairytale it was all because of God's healing power and grace.

Rain remembers the very night that Chase asked her to be his girlfriend. She looked a hot mess, her hair was unkempt, she was in her PJ's and they were on a FaceTime call. Chase looked like he was ready for the day, even though it was night time. He looked so handsome, his piercing blue eyes got brighter as he stared at her through the screen between them. The conversation was heavy as she opened up to him about the night she was raped. Tears flowed on both ends, Chase knew that this was what she experienced, but to hear her explain what happened in detail, made him angry to the point of tears. He was going to be there for her no matter what and help her through the healing process.

"Rain", he whispered, "You know I like you and I hate to see you cry." "You helped me heal in the hospital and I would like to help you continue to do the same." "Rain, would you be my girlfriend?" he added.

Rain hesitated as first, then spoke. "Chase, getting to know more about you outside the hospital, has been the best thing that's ever happen to me. Your family, welcoming me, as your friend and your dad offering me a job at his gallery, I am very grateful. I like you too Chase, as she looked into his piercing blue eyes through the screen, and yes, I will be your girlfriend." She added smiling.

Chase felt like he was going to jump out of his skin he was so excited that she was going to be his girlfriend, not just a friend anymore. He couldn't wait to take her on dates and show her what a real gentleman was like.

Rain, on the other hand, couldn't believe that she was actually going to be Chase's girlfriend. She dreamt about this day ever since leaving the hospital and now it finally was happening. She was blessed to be able to call him her boyfriend now and couldn't wait to see what the future held for their relationship.

"Good night, my darling". Chase said endearingly. "I want to take you out tomorrow, for our official first date, is that okay?" He asked.

"Good night, my handsome boyfriend, she said emphasizing the word 'boyfriend'. Of course, I would love to out go with you tomorrow." She added.

"Alrighty then, I will pick you up at noon, I have a

special day planned for our first date." He gushed and blew her a kiss through the screen.

She blew a kiss back to him and said "Good night, my dear," Then pushed the 'call end' button on her tablet.

After she ended her call with Chase, she climbed under the covers in her bed. She will dream of this night and of her handsome blue-eyed boyfriend. Chase who seems to stare straight into her soul every time he looks at her, had a way of knowing her thoughts and connecting with her on a spiritual level. She prayed before her eyes drifted to sleep, she thanked God for Chase and this exciting new chapter in their lives.

The next morning, she woke up excited to tell her mother the news that Chase was now her boyfriend and that their first official date was this afternoon. She got her shower and got dressed. She opted for a pink and purple butterfly printed, bell sleeved top and dark colored flare jeans. She decided to wear her pink flats, just in case they had to walk a lot. In her hair, newly washed, in the shower, she put her famous butterfly clip in, pulling back a few tight ringlets. She didn't know what Chase had planned for their first date, but she didn't care, as long as she was with him.

She rushed downstairs to the kitchen to see if her mom was in there making breakfast like she normally does on a Saturday. Her mother, still dressed in her PJ's with an apron on, was at the stove making the eggs, when Rain snuck up behind her.

"RAIN..." her mother jumped, "you almost made me spill these eggs." she exclaimed.

"Sorry, I'm sorry... Mom guess what?" She said excitingly.

"What? What?" Her mom echoed her excitement.

"Chase asked me to be his girlfriend and I said yes!" She gushed.

"Oh honey, that's wonderful, I just love Chase and I know he likes you. This makes me so happy. So when are you guys planning your first official date?" She asked.

"It's this afternoon, but I don't know where he's taking me". Rain told her mother.

"How's exciting, I'm sure you'll love and enjoy wherever he takes you". Her mother said smiling.

"Do you like what I'm wearing now? This is my date outfit." Rain asked her mother.

Her mother looked her daughter up and down and told her to 'do a spin'. Finally saying "Your outfit is perfect, Chase will surely love it as well."

"'You sure?" Rain asked.

"I'm positive." Her mother told her reassuringly.

"What time is Chase do to arrive?" Her mom asked

"Around noon." Rain said excitingly.

"Here, eat some breakfast. I made eggs, pancakes, bacon, cream of wheat and toast".

"Thanks, mom. I think I will" Rain said as she got up and fixed herself a plate.

As soon as Rain sat down at the table, she heard her dad's footsteps coming down the stairs.

"Honey, it smells so good, I'm starving." He gushed.

"Thanks, fix yourself a plate and come sit." She motioned to him." What's your plans for today, Micah?" She added.

"Well, I'm going to get my hair cut and go golfing with a few of the guys from work". He said.

"Oh, ok. Rain has a date." She told her husband

"Mom," Rain interjected

"Oh really? It's with Chase right? How are you two doing?" he asked

"Yes, it's with Chase, we're doing great, he asked me to be his girlfriend last night and I said yes." She told him.

"Oh really, it's that serious, maybe I should have a talk with Chase?" He questioned.

"No dad, I mean...when he wants to talk to you, he'll talk to you. Right now it's just the beginning stages, don't put too much pressure on him." She stated.

"Ok, ok, don't worry, I won't." He reassured her.

"Thank you, dad." She said relieved. "Because he's coming to pick me up at noon and I don't want you hounding him." She added.

"Honey, I told you I won't, I won't, I promise". He explained to her. "I'm leaving soon anyways, I have to go to meet the guys." He added.

"Have a great time golfing with your work friends." She said.

"Thanks Hon," he said as he was finishing up his plate of food. "Sade, I'm going to leave now, I have to meet them at the golf course at 11am. When I get back, would you like to go to have a late lunch?" He asked.

"Of course Micah, I would love that."

"Ok then, I will see you when I get back." He said to his wife.

"Rain, have a great date with Chase this afternoon."He told her as he was heading out the door.

"Thanks I will." She gushed.

She turned to her mother and said, "So you have a date as well". She said smiling.

"Yes, honey, I guess I do" she said laughing.

"Well, have fun on your date with dad". She added.

"Oh, I plan to," she said smirking.

"Well, I'm going to freshen up before Chase gets here". She said excusing herself from the table.

"Of course honey." She stated as she started to clean up the kitchen.

Rain went to her 'sanctuary', also known as her room. She had new drawings/paintings on her wall and a new 'work in progress' on her easel. The new work in process was a painting of Chase, in which she wanted to surprise him with it whenever she finished. Her journal, almost filled now, is a diary of the last few months outside the hospital getting to know Chase better. Her last entry was last night when Chase asked her to be his girlfriend. She put the journal back in the bin under her bed and then went into the bathroom to freshen up. She fixed her hair, brushed her teeth again and sprayed on her new perfume. She was date day ready, and she couldn't wait to see what Chase was wearing.

As soon as she finished, she rushed back downstairs into the living room and sat down on the couch to watch TV. She started to flip through the channels and didn't see too much that interested her. Her mom was still in the kitchen cleaning up after their big breakfast this morning.

"Do you need any help mom?" She asked.

"No, honey, I'm almost finished". She said looking out the window, as she spotted Chase walking up the driveway to the front door.

"Rain, get the door please" she asked.

Rain got up off of the couch, went to the door and opened it. There stood Chase, in black slacks and a buttoned down shirt. His hair was disheveled (just the way Rain liked it) and he smelled of expensive cologne.

Rain gave him the biggest smile as he handed her the red roses he brought.

"Here, darling. these are for you". He said, kissing her lightly on the lips.

Even though it was a light kiss on her lips, it took her breath away. It was the first time that they ever kissed.

"Thank you, they are beautiful." She said still memorized by his kiss.

"Are you ready to go?" He asked.

"Sure," she answered him. "Mom, We're getting ready to leave." she said as peeked in the doorway.

"Ok, honey, have fun", her mom said "Hi Chase".

"Hi, Mrs Thompson. See you soon". He answered.

Chase and Rain both walked to his car, he opened the passenger door for Rain and closed the door once she was safely inside. He then proceeded to the driver's side, opened the door, smiling at Rain, as to almost want to kiss her again. He climbed in, closed the door, made sure his and her seatbelt was secure, started the engine and then they were off.

"Where are we going?" Rain asked Chase politely

"I'm taking you to the skating rink and then we'll go get ice cream later at the local diner. Sounds good?" He asked looking at her, mesmerized by how beautiful she was and looked this afternoon.

"Sounds perfect!" Rain gushed. "As long as I'm with you, it doesn't really matter what we do". She said reaching over and playing in his hair. "I just love your disheveled hair". she added coyly.

He quickly smiled back at her, when she spoke about his hair, but kept his eyes on the road.

Rain sat nervously, excited to finally be on the first official date as boyfriend and girlfriend. Yes, they spent alone time together, but that was all in the confines of a hospital. This time they were able to explore and make different lasting memories together.

Soon they arrived at the skating rink. Chase found a decent parking space, he got out and opened the passenger door for Rain. As he let her out of the car, he brushed her hair with his hand and whispered in her ear, that she looked beautiful this afternoon. Rain gave him a shy smile and slightly blushed. He then interlocked his hand with hers and they headed inside the skating rink.

"Chase, it's been a while since I went skating". Rain explained.

"Don't worry, I've got you, I won't let you fall," He said with confidence.

"Ok, Chase, I'm trusting you," she said hesitantly.

The skating rink was packed with people, young and old alike. There were children's parties going on simultaneously.

Groups of high schoolers performing or trying to perform skating tricks. Then their were the seniors, sitting on the sidelines watching the younger crowd, possibly reminiscing of their younger, youthful years.

Chase paid for both him and Rain and they both went over to get their skates.

"Now are you sure you got this and me," Rain asked again.

"Rain, trust me, I got you." He said as he leaned over and kissed her. This kiss was slightly deeper and more engaging, the prior kiss on Rain's front door step. She took in the strong scent of his cologne, as he was kissing her.

He pulled away from her slowly and gave her a big smile. They got their skates and sat down at the nearest bench to lace them up.

"Are you ready?" Chase asked her.

"As ready as I'll ever be". She stated.

They both got up off the bench and stood up slowly. Rain stood up wobbly, Chase was there to guide her to the skating floor. He took her hand as they slowly went to the floor. The music, some techno mashup was playing over the loud speaker as they went carefully around the circular rink. The strobe lights, a rainbow of colors flashed around, shining on various people as they skated around the rink.

"Are you ok?" Chase asked Rain as they skated around the rink a few times.

"Yes, I'm ok." She told him.

"Do you want to try on your own, without me holding your hand?" He asked.

"Ummm...not really," she confessed.

"Ok, I got you, don't worry". He reassured her.

They skated around the rink a couple more times when they collectively decided that it was time to leave. Chase helped Rain back to the bench they sat down at earlier. They each untied their skates, took them off and went to hand them in.

They then left the rink, got back in Chase's car and headed to the local diner for ice cream. Inside the diner, they chose to sit at a booth, for more privacy. Upon sitting down, Chase asked the waiter for two dessert menus. As they were waiting for the menus, they discussed how the first official date went.

"You were okay with holding my hand the entire time while I was skating, Chase?" Rain questioned him.

"Yes, of course, why would you question that? I loved being in close proximity with you. I could hold your hand forever," he gushed. "Babe, listen I'm not like the guys in your past, don't worry about being afraid to say what's on your mind and if I'm in any way moving too fast for you, you can tell me," he explained

"Ok", she said knowing what past 'guy' he was talking about.

Soon after, the waiter brought over the two dessert menus. Chase asked how big the banana split was and if it was enough for two people. The waiter explained the portion size and they both agreed to share one banana split. The waiter collected their menus and went to put in the order.

"Chase, can I ask you a question? Since you know my

history. Forgive me if this is too forward, but have you ever had sex before?" Rain asked.

"No worries, Rain. Unfortunately, I have had sex before. I didn't know what I know now and how damaging it was for both her and I. You have to understand, I came from a broken home, I know that's no excuse. But I repented and I know better now." He explained.

"Thanks for your honesty, I appreciate it" Rain stated.

"Your welcome. You don't have to worry, Rain. We are going to wait and when we are ready, I will ease your mind, heart and soul. You won't have to be afraid, I will not take advantage of you. I like you too much to do that. Do you trust me?" He said sincerely.

"Yes, I trust you," she said as she squeezed his hand endearingly.

Just then, the waiter arrived with their banana split and two spoons. Both Chase and Rain each grabbed one of the spoons and dug into the ice cream.

Ebonee:

My motivation for completing this novel.

Thank you for pushing me to finish what I started in 2014.

Jenna B. Neece:

Thank you for editing and fine tuning 'ALITPW'. Thank you for believing in me as an author.

Diana TC:

Thank you so much for making me an EPIC cover design.

To Kacey Kells:

Thank you for your friendship. You are a brave and amazing woman. I'm still in shock that you follow me on Twitter, when I secretly waited and wanted you to follow me back. I only hope I can meet you one day.

To #WritingCommunity (Twitter):

There are too many of you to name one by one. But I just want to thank you all for accepting me into an awesome bunch of creatives. I love you all and wish you much success in all your writing endeavors.

ABOUT THE AUTHOR

Regina Ann Faith *is a Lyricist, Poet, Writer, Composer and Author. She graduated with a B.A in Communications/Film. She has been writing since she was a teenager and grew up wanting to write as a career. Her Novella is a New Adult Romance entitled "Artistic Love In The Psych Ward". It deals with death, sexual assault, physical abuse, friendship and the healing process. Although, fictional, the novella is loosely based on her past experiences with anxiety and depression.*

She can be found on her social media pages at:

www.facebook.com/ArtisticBookSeries

www.twitter.com/ReginaAnnFaith

www.instagram.com/ReginaAnnFaith

www.soundcloud.com/ReginaAnnFaith

www.youtube.com/ReginaAnnFaithMusic

Printed in Great Britain
by Amazon

82358152R00072